The Priest and The Assassin

A Father Mike Novel

by

T.R. HANEY

authorHOUSE®

AuthorHouse™
1663 Liberty Drive, Suite 200
Bloomington, IN 47403
www.authorhouse.com
Phone: 1-800-839-8640

First published by AuthorHouse 7/16/2008

ISBN: 978-1-4389-0509-9 (e)
ISBN: 978-1-4343-9553-5 (sc)

Cover Design by Curt Rohrer

Printed in the United States of America
Bloomington, Indiana

This book is printed on acid-free paper.

1

"Word on the street is Charon is out to get you, Father Mike."

I sit staring at Scuds. He is a wiry little man. His face is gray like a slice of winter sun. His eyes are so close he could pass for a Cyclops. A long nose hung from his forehead like a rope ready to be made into a hangman's noose. He isn't easy to look at.

His clothes look like they're on a clothes hanger. Shabby and dirty. There is nothing appealing about him. He falls into that category called tolerated.

He's the town crier on Forrow Street. I don't know what his nickname means. He's always just been Scuds, living on the street for years. But he's usually well informed.

I give him food now and then and some hand-me-down clothes. So he feels obligated to dump the current gossip into my worn ears. I always hate to hear his gossip. I take people's problems too personally.

But this time it's different. It's about me. About my murder, to be more precise.

"Charon, the assassin?" I ask.

"The same," Scuds says back to me. "He a mean one, he is. Too mean to die."

"Too mean to die?" I repeat Scuds' words in question form, hoping for clarification.

"That's the way they put it out on the street," says Scuds. 'Too mean to die.' He was shot three time onct. And now he's up and around. He a mean cat. Gots nine lives."

"Why are you telling me this?" I ask.

" 'Cause they say he's after you.

" 'Member Joey Cortello? You helped put him away. He's Charon's boyfriend, if you get my meaning."

"Yes," I say, knowing full well that Scuds is telling me that the infamous assassin, Charon, is gay. And they say the Trinity's a mystery! A blood thirsty, maniacal killer gay? God's menagerie.

"He's in Chicago now?" I ask.

"Yep. You ain't got no chance," says Scuds. "He too mean to die. He kill you 'fore you can do anythin'.

"Well," I say, "thanks for telling me this, Scuds."

He smiles with satisfaction like the proverbial Cheshire cat and leaves. Rather he leaves me shuddering, to be more precise.

I check my computer, more out of curiosity than research. I want to know what the name, Charon, means.

And there it is: Charon: a son of Erebus who in Greek mythology ferries the souls of the dead over the river Acheron, not the Styx as sometimes stated

I don't know who gave him this name, but I really don't care. But it's more than a name. It's a prophecy.

I suppose the proper response to prophecy is prayer. But prayer is the least of my desires right now. Perhaps I whisper a 'God help me,' but that's it.

God helps those who help themselves. How often I've said that? And now I must live it if I have any faith at all.

Why do those of us who are trying to fulfill God's purpose, his dream for us, get so tangled in trials, so scalded with anxiety, so caught in the jaws of suffering?

I don't know and now's not the time to ponder. I've got to do something. What? I haven't the slightest idea. Once again, I do whisper, "God help me."

I do believe that the sign of the cross makes sense only when we make it a sign of personal crucifixion.

The proof of Jesus commitment is not that he was nailed to a cross in total powerlessness, but that he refused to use his infinite power to come down from the cross.

2

Actually things are going smoothly here at this upscale parish of St. Ignatius over the past two years. Much better than I had anticipated. Many of my former poorer parishioners from St. Malachy's now sit on various parish committees.

I am pleasantly surprised that the people of St. Ignatius have taken a black pastor into their hearts. They support me almost unconditionally. Although they think, my guess, that I'm a bit quirky the way I get involved in matters of crime fighting.

But that's the way it is. I am happy.

Not to denigrate my predecessor, Bibi, but he was more of a distant administrator, very efficient but very withdrawn. Not involved in people's lives and problems.

Bibi's a good priest who runs a business.

The Cardinal was right. People who are upward mobile and well off and successful do have their own kind of poverty: lack of self-esteem, dissatisfied despite owning a lot of things, gaps in marital relationships, fretting over spoiled children, despondency and alcoholism. The list goes on and on. And the well-to-do people are in desperate need of the healing touch of affirmation.

I have my own problem. I'm probably too involved, taking people's problems too deeply into my heart, torturing myself endlessly like a suicidal masochist.

I remember when I was a young priest, telling my mother about all the problems I hear in the office. And how I go up to my room and sit there so depressed.

She says to me, "People tell you their problems and you to your room worried sick. They go home whistling. Does that make sense?"

A maternal oversimplification but it does help me to change my focus a bit.

The problem is the balance between being empathetic and being distantly clinical. Like most priests, I have to keep in mind that the individual sitting in front of me is a person to be respected not a problem to be solved.

And now this!

I'm thinking I have to take Scuds' report literally. A professional hit man is gunning or whatever for me.

The story of Joey Cortello wasn't all that noticeable. Joey, a slight wisp of a man, with knotted hair and pock marked face is a small time thief. The police ask my help. They ask me to let it be known that a lot of money was being put into our parish poor box. Far more than is true.

Two policemen sit in church waiting, hoping Joey would hear about my announcement. It would be his kind of heist. I wonder if the policemen pray while they are sitting in the back pew.

Then Joey indeed shows up. As he is being apprehended, he pulls out a gun and shoots one of the policemen dead. Thus his life sentence.

I couldn't understand why the police were so interested in catching Joey. But now that I heard what Scuds said about Joey's relationship with Charon, I understand.

They were using Joey for bait. They knew his relationship with Charon. They were hoping Charon would try to rescue his lover. Nothing. Except that now Charon was after me.

Why Joey was stealing, I don't know. I would think that Charon would have taken very good care of him. Maybe Joey was just addicted. Maybe it was the thrill of getting away with it. Maybe Charon is a selfish lover.

But then if he is, why would he want my scalp?

Tonight I go to my room worried sick but nobody's whistling.

3

I am reading up on world famous or infamous assassins like Carlos and The Jackal.

No doubt Charon fits in with them. From the little I hear of him, he's not just a hired hit man. He's a psychopathic killer, a loose canon on the ship of civilization.

The police throughout the world know about him. But they can never find him. He's a shadow slipping in and out of the sunrays. Now he's here killing someone, now he's gone. Poof! No one knows *who* he is, just *that* he is.

Some assassins are hired full time by an organization. Some are freelancers. And, yes, some work for our own Government. They are very adept at disguises and this is why they are also professional escapees.

Assassins are sociopaths. They have no sense of right or wrong. No conscience. For them there just isn't any morality. There is no empathy when they are sanctioning someone. No remorse afterward. Still they can be charming and engaging.

Assassins have fractured psyches. On the one hand, they are organized stone cold killers. On the other hand, they may also have a disorganized sexual sadism charged with rage.

When both sides of their psyches merge, they will be criminals with the skills and efficiency of master assassins and the rage of suicide bombers.

One day they will explode. And God help those around them on that day.

What they do is just a matter of a job like an insurance agent going to work each day. Depending on their record and reputation, hit men or women can make anywhere from a few hundred dollars to fifty or hundreds of thousands a sanction.

I read somewhere about one female assassin who got a million dollars per.

The exception, of course, are those who work for a government. They're salaried. They rationalize what they do as their patriotic duty. And their superiors rationalize the sanctions they order as being done for that slippery phrase, National Security, or just the good order of things.

It's the timeworn bromide, "I was just following orders." The universal excuse for all kinds of atrocities. And agencies within our Government lie and deceive as a matter of policy even to their own agents. They rationalize this too.

I'm beginning to imagine myself standing at the altar or pulpit and being shot to death. Or walking down the street or coming out of a home or hospital after visiting the sick and shut-ins.

One thing that is not a product of my imagination is that Charon is out to get me.

What to do?

If I contact the police, they'll invoke the principle of hearsay and tell me there's nothing they can do. Nothing unless I'm shot. Shot to death. They'll say Scuds' report to me is just the paranoid ranting of a wino, hallucinations passed off as facts.

Anyway, they'd say, a professional never takes anybody out without being paid. Oh, good, now maybe somebody has put out a contract on me. Paranoid? Why not?

I feel like I'm doing a jig through a minefield. Maybe I'll go see Don Giovanni.

Why is it that Easter joy so quickly reverts to the suffering of the Passion? The nails of crucifixion are never far from our hands.

4

While I am sitting at my desk, heavy oak as opposed to the tin thing I had at St. Malachy's, my secretary, Mrs. Fromm, who followed me to St. Ignatius, tapped on the door.

"Logan Helfry is here for his appointment." She always pronounced the young man's name as Log-on like in a computer. Why? I don't know and I won't ask either.

Logan stands six feet nine. He is well built. His skin is dark, not like an Eight Ball, more like light chocolate. He is handsome in a rugged sort of way. He moves as smoothly as a panther.

He comes into my office and stands until I invite him to sit.

"Father Mike," he says softly as he sits down.

"Logan," I say back. "It's good to see you."

Logan sits silently. I realize I am to start the conversation.

"Well, what can I do for you, Logan?" I ask smiling my best PR smile, hoping I don't look like a ninny.

"I'm thinking of leaving school," he says matter of factly.

"You're a junior?" I ask, knowing I'm right.

"Yes," Logan responds with a heavy sigh.

"And the reason is …?":

"I'm sick and tired of being hassled. Especially by the basketball coach. But everybody's doing it. 'How come you don't go out for basketball?' It's like the refrain in a song, over and over.

"Then I get, 'You afraid you get hurt?' 'You chicken?' 'Hey, you're six nine, we could use you.' That from the coach."

I sit waiting for more.

"You know, Father Mike, that I am close to being a concert pianist. Music's my whole life. So I'm supposed to go out for basketball and risk getting a finger broken? Maybe a shoulder smashed. Any potential as a concert pianist gone. For what? A lousy cheer?"

"Logan," I say, "being hassled is no reason to quit school." Then I feel like I've just uttered the bromide of all bromides.

"You don't have to go through it every day," Logan says.

Oh no! I think. What about being hassled by an assassin?

"Logan," I say, "I want to ask you some questions. You don't have to answer them right now. I want you to think about them prayerfully."

He nods his head.

"Do you believe in yourself? Do you have enough self-esteem that you can deflect the harassment you're getting for not playing basketball? What is your goal in life and how willing are you to sacrifice for it, not just practicing the piano but overcoming the sneers from others? Do you want recognition for your God-given gift?"

Logan sits there apparently absorbing these questions.

"Logan," I say, "do you remember the story of Goliath and David?" I ask, realizing my metaphor has a gaping hole since Logan is six foot nine. But then Goliath was a giant. He could have been ten feet tall. So I'm going to push it.

"Yes," he answers.

"Well, we all have Goliaths in our lives. They're obstacles that seem too big to face up to or too powerful to overcome. But God gives us the power, strength and courage to defeat our Goliaths if we tap into the power he gives us.

"Your Goliath right now is the negative attitude and remarks others are making to you. Now you can run away in fear, drop out of school, become withdrawn and isolated. Or you can stand up to your Goliath and defeat him by braving all the snide remarks and sloughing them off.

"Consider the source. The kids who are bedeviling you probably have no idea what they want to do with their lives. They're just living for the next game or dance or party. You are so far ahead of them, so far above them, not only in physical height but in character, why should you care what they think or say?"

The silence, as they say, is deafening. We sit there for a couple of minutes which seem like hours saying nothing.

Then Logan says, "You're right, Father Mike. I guess I just needed to hear someone say what you just said."

With that he gets up, smiles and embraces me against his huge body and leaves.

I sit there hoping and praying that he will make the right choices. Not all problems are that easy. Some lead to the edge of despair. I wonder if Logan is going home whistling.

5

He moves around the kitchen as if it were a foreign land yet to be explored. He moves gingerly as if he would break something just by touching it.

He stands six feet three inches at two hundred and thirty pounds of pure muscle from working out for hours each day.

His face wears a perpetual scowl, his eyes are as dark as a grave. He is balding slightly but a handsome man. Yet for all his bulk, his fingers are as slim and facile as a surgeon's. Perfect for the life work he has chosen.

His culinary skills are limited to making coffee and scrambling eggs. And that is what he is doing, scrambling six eggs – and burning them.

Joey did all the cooking.

He misses Joey. Damn that priest!

The phone rings.

"Oh, Hi, Mom," he says in the most congenial tone. "I know, I missed Christmas but I had business to attend to. He doesn't tell her his business was taking out a member of the English Parliament who was causing a raucous over the peace treaty in Ireland.

He always finds out who hires him and they know if they don't fulfill the contract, they're next on his hit list. It happened just once and the word spread like a wild fire.

"Yes I know your birthday is in two months and I plan to be there," he almost whimpered. "Okay, Mom, and I love you too."

By now the eggs are good for nothing but to be thrown out.

He sits at the table sipping some rancid coffee. The phone rings again.

He recognizes the voice immediately. It's his contact.

Charon never meets his clients. He's contacted through his surrogates.

"No, I can't take a job then. I have a very important engagement." He doesn't tell his contact that it is his mother's birthday. He doesn't even want anyone to know he has a mother.

"One million!" he exclaims. He could take the job and be just a little late for his mother's birthday.

"All right," he says. Same set up. Five hundred thousand before and the same after the job's done. Have the 'client' send the info to my PO Box."

The phone number and PO Box address is all his contact knows. Except, of course, that his contact knows he's Charon. But his contact couldn't pick him out of a crowd even if he was wearing an ID badge.

He hangs up and hums a bit. It's only the second time he is being paid one million dollars for a job. Usually it's somewhere between a quarter and a half million. He never counts the number of jobs he's performed. No need to. But he knows his Swiss account is bulging.

He could have retired years ago. But he likes the rush he gets from the jobs. The minute preparations, the immediate anticipation, the strike, the closure. Any hunter could identify.

He goes back to scrambling some more eggs. He surely misses Joey.

6

About two weeks after Scud's visit, the police call me out on an emergency. Even though I am now in a "better" part of town, the police still call on me.

Sometimes, like this, the emergency isn't even in my parish boundaries. This emergency is down in the heart of the city.

Most of the time, I don't even know if the victims are Catholic, so I give conditional absolution and anointing.

For the past weeks, I am envisioning all kinds of scenarios like standing at the altar or in the pulpit and being shot dead.

I visit Don Giovanni and tell him what Scuds tells me.

"Charon?" Don Giovanni says. "He's a mean one. I never use him. I have my own, shall we say, accommodations. He's in Chicago now?" he asks.

"According to Scuds he is," I tell him.

"I don't know how I can protect you, Father Mike," he says wistfully. "I can tell my boys to keep an eye out, but this guy is as slippery as mercury. He's like The Shadow."

I don't feel any better. But I can tell you. I feel like a target in a shooting gallery at a carnival.

I arrive downtown and am greeted by Detectives Paul Morissey and Alison Masconi.

Detective Hassler retired some time after Father Jim had been arrested.

Detective Morissey is a short, heavy set man in his fifties He's balding and paunchy. He is, in a word, sloppy. His clothes hang slovenly on him. He's laid back, calm and almost indifferent as though he's been through this stuff so many times it doesn't even register anymore. But his demeanor belies the keenness of intellect that I'd come to know over the years. His eyes are beams of observation and perception.

Detective Masconi is tall, almost to the point of being lanky. Her brownish hair is severely pulled back into a knot. She looks like she should be playing in professional women's basketball. She's not pretty but she's not homely either. I guess you'd say she's handsome. Attractive in a drag sort of way. She does have a disarming smile which immediately designates her as the "good guy." Her eyes are wide and roving.

She's relatively new on the job and you can feel the electricity of her excitement. Morissey introduces her to me. I'm sure she's a match for her partner.

Detective Morissey says to me in a tone as low as a shy child asking for another cookie, "It's looks like a professional hit, Father Mike."

I look at the gaping hole in the man's forehead. The angle indicates that he was shot from a height like from one of the buildings across the street.

I kneel and give him conditional absolution and anoint him conditionally.

"Do you know who he is?" I ask as I straighten up.

"His name is Charles Sterling," Detective Masconi answers enthusiastically as though she has just solved a puzzle. "According to what's in his wallet, he's the Senior Vice President of Bradford and Bradford. Octogenics. Apparently he was coming out of their building there and heading for his limo when he got hit."

Detective Masconi pauses as though she's wondering why she is telling me all this.

"You'll have to do some digging to find out what he was up to," I say as I survey the street and the buildings around.

"Obviously somebody wanted him out of the way for something," Detective Masconi shrugs. Detective Morissey just stands there with his hands in his pockets looking like he'd like to go for a cup of coffee or a cold beer, even though it's still morning.

"Well," I say to Detective Morissey, "if you find out anything, let me know."

I make my way back to the rectory, wondering who the hit man is and feeling pretty sure I know. I am shaking. A prophecy fulfilled in our midst.

I wash some dishes crowded into the sink. Ever since Mrs. Mortle had her stroke, I've been doing my own cooking and cleaning. My Parochial Vicar doesn't seem to mind my cooking but he doesn't mind not helping with the dishes either.

He's a fine young man. Conscientious to a fault, hard working and pious.

I'm blessed, even if he isn't domesticated.

7

Two days later Detective Morissey calls me.

"Hi, Father Mike," he says in his usual droning tone. "I got info for you if you're interested."

"Info about what," I ask.

"About Charles Sterling, the guy who was assassinated."

The word, assassinated, set me on edge. "It was an assassination, then?" I ask.

"No doubt. Like you know he was the Senior Vice President of Bradford and Bradford Octogenic Chemicals..

"That part I do know."

"Now the info we got is that his conglomerate is under investigation by the Securities and Exchange Commission alleging multiple violations involving billions of dollars in illegal transactions. Octogenics is a huge multinational with annual sales of twenty to thirty billion dollars . Apparently Sterling made an appointment to speak to members of the Securities and Exchange Commission Department ..."

"He was a whistle blower," I say.

"Yeah, and somebody didn't like the tune he was whistling, didn't want him talkin' to anybody. So our research tells us."

"So it was probably a paid assassin who did the job," I say, hoping it isn't true.

"Most likely," Morissey says with no emotion.

"Any idea who the assassin might be?"

"They say Charon's in town. Could be him. The telltale chewing wrapper was left behind. Could be him or a wanna-be."

"Any chance of tracking him down?"

"Probably not, if it's him. There are a few others of them assassins around."

But only one Charon, I'm thinking.

"Remember Joey Cortello?" I ask.

"Yep. I wasn't in on that one but I heard all about it. Used him for bait to get Charon. Fell through. Now Joey's in for life."

"Any chance Charon might go after the ones who set Joey up?"

"Don't know. Charon's crazy enough to try a stunt like that. The cops involved have been warned to be on the alert."

"Detective Morissey, there's something I need to tell you."

"What's that, Father Mike?"

I told him what Scuds had told me. And the part I played in the capture of Joey.

"Could be true," again without the slightest sign of concern.

"What do you think I should do?"

"Don't know. Let me think about it for a while."

"Okay," I say with about as much relief as someone having a truck bearing down on him.

With that we disconnected.

3

I guess we all put thoughts of our own deaths on the back burner. Not so much out of fear but because, if we dwell on our death too much, we'll live life in total morbidity. The walking dead, kind of.

Yet the only way to live life fully is to embrace the fact of death. As a priest, I pray each day during the Eucharist, "... protect us from all anxiety as we wait in joyful hope for the coming of our savior, Jesus Christ."

Real faith, not just the words by rote, recognizes that Jesus' coming at our death is a joyful occasion. A time for dynamic hope in the infinite mercy of God.

All this is great theory until you hear there's somebody out there drawing a bead on you. An assassin in waiting. And you're the target running around until he gets you in his sights.

I read somewhere that because of the infinite redemptive merits of Jesus, God has already forgiven us every evil we *will* ever do. He does not even wait for us to commit a sin. His forgiveness has already been given to us.

With this realization there is no room for fear or despair. No reason to rationalize our sinfulness. All we have to do is accept the lavish mercy and the all-embracing forgiveness God is already extending to us by repenting of the sins that have separated or are separating us from him.

It's a thought that I am now drawing consolation from these days.

9

I go to see Jacob Reitz, an old retired priest, my sometime confessor. Tell him all. He shocks me. He laughs. A sort of chuckle. "Well, lad," he says to me, "if I were you, I'd make the best confession of my life and then go into hiding." (chuckle).

Thanks a lot. But I didn't say it.

"Look, Mike," he says, "there's really nothing you can do. There's a bullet with your name on it and it belongs to a professional shooter. Right now you're in your Garden of Gethsemane. You're sweating blood. Now is your prayer going to be, 'Not my will but yours be done'?"

It is interesting that God walked the garden with his first human beings. After the resurrection, he is spotted as the gardener in the new garden with his chosen ones.

He's right, of course. I make a confession going back to when I pulled wings off a fly and everything since. It is difficult since I'm not given to scrupulosity and I'm handy at rationalizing.

I don't feel relieved as I thought I would. No big burden off my back and things like that. I'm just as scared as when I came in.

Suddenly, old Jake begins to weep. "You're not only a good priest, Mike, you're a wonderful human being. I don't know why this is happening to you, but you must have faith – a fearless trust in God. You tirelessly give your daily service to the people of God.

"I don't know why God has let me live all these ninety-three years. Maybe it's to encourage men like you. You could come around oftener and confess more frequently. Bur don't go through a confession like this one again. God forgives you." (a tender smile).

I thank him for his words of affirmation. And we give each other a blessing. I leave telling him I will be around oftener.

10

The prospect if imminent death changes and focuses your whole perspective. You see how you've spent – or wasted –time on a lot of silly things.

You ask yourself important questions. Like, Have I been holding onto the message of Jesus but losing my experience of Jesus? And, as a result, has the zeal of my faith become the dullness of duty? How generously do I forgive 70 times 7 times? What does walking the extra mile really mean?

How do I live the Beatitudes and make them the standard of my spiritual growth? How intimately do I relate the gospel message to my everyday life? Is my prayer truly a friendly, honest, open communication with the God who lives within me?

I remember seeing an interview on television with Peter O'Toole. When asked what he wanted for an epitaph on his tombstone, he answered, "I would take it from a sign at the local cleaners: 'It distresses us to return work that is not perfect.'"

My sentiments exactly.

I go home and go over to church. I'm doing that a lot lately.

As I'm kneeling and praying, I remember an older priest who was sickly. Once he almost died. He said to me and a priest friend, "When you're at death's door and you come back, a lot of things you thought were important, aren't.".

11

Later I go looking for Scuds. I find him holding forth in a back alley with only one in the audience, and he's blitzed with booze.

"Scuds," I say to him, "keep your ear to the ground and let me know if Charon leaves town. Will you do that for me?"

Scuds bows his head in agreement. "I can't promise you nothing," he says.

"I need some breathing room, Scuds," I say to him. "This is really important, okay?"

"Okay," he says but he doesn't sound too confident.

Two days later, Scuds comes around.

"Word on the street," he says while munching on a Liverwurst sandwich I make for him, "is that Charon is now gone out of town."

"How do you get this information?" I ask him.

He just smiles.

12

FBI agent Sylvester Kerns is pacing back and forth, a cigarette in his hand, unlit.

He is tall. Over six three maybe. Thin and handsome except for the scar down his left cheek from a knife slice. His hair is thinning, emphasizing his brown eyes, now blazing with either anger or deep annoyance. His forehead is furrowed as if in an agonized thrashing of ideas.

"The damnable thing," Syl says, "is we don't have an iota of description. We don't know his nationality. We don't know anything."

"You're sure it's Charon?" his colleague, Jake Sesson, asks obviously concerned.

His shorter, more compact body contrasted with Syl, Jake looked like what he once was, an all star tackle for Notre Dame. He exudes strength except for his left leg which was broken in his final college game, ruining all the lucrative prospects for pro football. He is totally bald and ugly in an athletic sort of way. A broken nose and cheekbone hadn't helped.

"No doubt at all, Jake. The chewing gum wrapper. It's his signature. The arrogant bastard."

"How long you been chasing him?" Jake asks without showing much interest in an answer.

"Off and on, about four or five years, I guess. And I'm no closer than I was when I started." Syl answers, exhaling a frustrated sigh.

"Now I hear he's after a priest. You know him. That Father Mike who's helped solved some murders," Syl says without displaying much interest.

"He's the one," Jake said offhandedly, "who turned in one of his own, right?"

"The one of his own was guilty of killing a number of prostitutes. Looney bin as I understand it," Syl answers as he sits on the edge of his desk, still fidgeting with his unlit cigarette.

"Cops say this Charles Sterling who was taken out was planning some explosive revelations about the conglomerate," Jake says, getting up for another cup of coffee.

"You have to wonder why that would be reason enough to have him assassinated," Syl said more to himself than to Jake. "He must have had a hell've lot of info."

"Yeah," Jake responded, "and who would have a line to Charon to get him to terminate a guy like Charles Sterling. Where do you go from here?" It is Jake's turn for a heavy sigh.

"Where I always go – nowhere. We don't even have a physical description. The closest we came was his lover, Joey Cortello. The cops did a good job rounding him up. That's how the priest got involved. They used his church to set up a trap. I was in on it from a distance.

"We thought for sure that Charon would come and get his lover boy back."

"A guy like Charon has no feelings," Jake said, sounding a bit philosophical. "He's as dead inside as the people he terminates. With all due respect, the plan was a waste of effort. And then Joey shoots and kills a cop. Now Joey's as good as dead in prison."

"We keep trying to come up with whatever plans we can. It keeps hope alive. At least my hope," Syl sounded hopeless.

"What about the priest?" Jake asks.

"I guess the cops are handling that. I don't know how much can be done to protect him," Syl again sounded hopeless.

"How did the priest find out?" Jake asks.

"Some street guy told him."

"Reliable?"

"The priest seems to think so."

"What a mess." Now Jake sounds hopeless.

13

I sit in my study. It's about three times larger than the one I had at St. Malachy's. Dark wood paneling, red carpeting. A built in bar in the spacious bookcases that line two walls. A huge dark oak desk. Five easy chairs. Lamps that look antique. I don't know antique from old.

I still miss my sparse accommodations at St. Malachy's which is now a parsonage for a Black Baptist minister and his wife. A wonderful couple with whom I'm friends.

As a sign of good will and ecumenism, I suppose, they kept the name St. Malachy.

ST. MALACHY FIRST BAPTIST CHURCH.

Once again I find myself contemplating evil. Specifically the evil of an assassin. If an assassin is a psychopath, how does God judge the evil he's responsible for?

And is an assassin a psycho? Or did he or she make a conscious choice to make murder his occupation? But then how much moral training plays a part in such a decision? Is the assassin morally dead? If so, how responsible is he or she for the objective evil of murder?

Here I am preaching and teaching Christian morality, warning, motivating, challenging people to live the gospel values counterculturally and outside my venue a whole other group that has no sense of morality whatsoever.

It's the same with the prostitutes on Forrow Street. What are their moral standards? They're convinced that they're just offering a service that is needed. As one said to me, "Why give it away when you can charge for it?"

Is it a matter of morality or just a business, as they claim?

Then there are the ex prostitutes who are at Forrow Haven. The refuge Gloria Winthrop, the wealthy lawyer set up to rescue prostitutes off the street.

Gloria had had cancer and sadly died after a brief remission.

Gloria's funeral was city-wide celebration.

The Cardinal, the Mayor and other distinguished guests were in attendance.

On the other side of the aisle, sat the women from Forrow Haven. Behind them sat the women of the street all decked out in their alluring garb. Amazing.

Her mother was there but not her father.

I preached the homily. I praised Gloria as the Samaritan who stopped by Forrow Street and bound up the wounds of those who were in such desperate need.

I said that just as the story of the Good Samaritan changes consciousness and challenges us to become involved in the needs of others, so does Gloria's story.

I said Jesus defines compassion through this story and Gloria lived that compassion. I made several other statements about Gloria's heroic virtues.

I said that Gloria turned her cross of cancer into the resurrection of many women and young girls who had nowhere else to go.

Gloria rolled the stone of the past aside for these women and offered them new life.

I said that Gloria was truly a living saint even though she might never be canonized.

I kept it short according to Gloria's wishes.

Many in the congregation were openly weeping.

Christine Joyce, Lulu's sister --the detective whom Jim had mistakenly killed since she was working undercover as a prostitute -- was there. Christine has taken over Forrow Haven.

How do we distinguish between morality and mental illness? And are prostitutes and assassins really mentally ill? They function all right within society but when a certain button is pushed, they're no longer within the boundaries of society. Is that a kind of schizophrenia?

The assassin, as I understand it, is usually a loner, filled with resentment, hatred, vindictiveness. Perhaps battered by his father. Gets involved with a gang, learns all there is to know about firearms, joins the army, becomes an expert sniper and changes from a murderer to an executioner.

At least there has to be a certain lack of self worth and self esteem. How responsible are they for this lack?

To spot the seeds of resentment before they bloom into the fruit of bad behavior is essential.

It's so simple to say, This is a sin and that's a sin. But is sin a sin for everyone?

What about a prostitute who takes generous care of a brother or sister or a son or daughter for that matter?

Can there be a stifling of growth on the moral level when on other levels like the emotional, there is exceptional growth. Or in the case of assassins, the intellectual level? There are assassins who are well read in philosophy for example. And how can they read this stuff and not be influenced by it?

It's sort of like the parishioner who hears a homily and says, "I know just the person this applies to."

Moral standards must be accepted. They can't be imposed. Imposition doesn't guarantee internalization.

If immoral behavior is based on ignorance, wouldn't it be better not to know than to be schooled in moral doctrine?

I'm thinking of Jim now. He killed all those prostitutes but obviously he isn't responsible, being mentally ill so much so that he actually thought he was doing something good.

14

Next my thoughts turn to where they have been almost as incessantly as the chimes in the Grandfather clock BB left behind. (Probably bought it with parish funds).

The thoughts about death. My death to be more specific.

I wonder what the judgment would really be like.

Someone said the best preparation for death is to increase your sense of surprise.

What surprises would God have in store?

Then I dwell for a while on something I try not to. What if all we've been taught about the afterlife is just guesswork.

No one really knows.

Oh, we have descriptions like the goats on one side and the sheep on the other. And we know that we'll be judged by how we related to one another. Surprisingly, not by how many Masses we celebrated or how many prayers we said or how many sacrifices. But whether or not we treated each person as we would treat Christ.

But what if …

This comes down to the very roots of faith.

We have to believe what is recorded in the gospel and what the Church teaches us.

After all, faith is belief without proof.

From my readings in process theology, I have decided that the afterlife is not eternal rest but the continuing growth and development, begun here and going on for all eternity.

That would certainly be a surprise when you consider all the times we prayed that eternal rest would be granted to the deceased.

Death may well be an entering into a new creative energy.

In my reading I came across an idea that has stuck with me: Death is just one moment in the process of our becoming.

After all we are not a blind glob of protoplasm. We are creatures who live in a world of symbols. We are people of self worth with a name and a history. The afterlife must preserve this. And in the afterlife we can continue our historic development.

In the afterlife, we will be totally free to continue to develop. No more restrictions as there are in this life. No more struggle. No more downsides. No more failures. Death is ultimate freedom.

In Process theology, experience means change. If there is no change after death (eternal rest) there is no ongoing experience. If we continue to experience God in heaven, then we continue to change. And we change for the best. In other words we continue to grow and develop, becoming more and more of who we are – eternally becoming.

This makes sense when you think that we only use about 10% of our mental ability during our lifetime. There is so much more room for our development in the next life.

That's what I'm thinking anyhow as I face the probability of my own death.

Yet, I suppose, if the assassin should take me out, I will feel cheated. There is so much more I want to do, so many people I want to help. But that's not my call, is it?

I must believe that I am unique. No one like me ever existed before and no one like me will ever exist again. That uniqueness must be preserved some way somehow.

For now I have a sneaking suspicion that I am afraid. Fear comes from the need to control. And there is no controlling of death except perhaps in suicides. There is certainly no controlling the afterlife. That's for sure.

I kneel down at my prie-dieu and ask God to increase my faith in his infinite mercy and love. I ponder the image of the Good Shepherd. I tell God that I am the lost coin and ask him to find me and keep me forever.

I must offer this prayer often, I know.

15

I have appointment to see the Cardinal.

I feel that I owe it to him to tell him about this threat on my life.

I don't want him to remove me and send me into hiding. I much rather die in the midst of the action than be buried alive somewhere safe, still waiting for the assassin to find me which undoubtedly he would.

Yesterday I called Monsignor Bevins, the Cardinal's secretary, for an appointment.

Typical of his snooty manner, he tries to put me through an inquisition as to why I want an appointment.

He can't refuse me an appointment. It's just a matter of his trying to satisfy his curiosity. He has to be in on the know. Of course, he could give me an appointment for a month from now. He does have that tiny drop of power.

I tell him, "It's a matter of life or death."

That got his full, imperial attention. "May I ask whose life or death," he asked, sounding that he is hoping it's mine. He's never forgiven me for calling him an ass.

16

"Your credentials are very impressive," the Warden says to the applicant for the job as a guard at the Federal prison.

Charon smiled to himself. Fiction is more 'impressive' than fact.

"When can you start?" the Warden asks.

"Tomorrow," Charon answers.

"Fine, see Smathers for your work detail today."

The next day Charon, dressed in his guard uniform, is making his rounds. He walks out into the yard and runs into his lover, Joey Cortello.

"Charon," Joey whispers, "am I glad to see you. You come to get me out?"

"Yes, Joey. I come to get you out."

"Thank whatever god is smiling on me this day," Joey's voice is a little louder.

"Shhh," Charon instructs. "Just pretend I'm checking you out."

With that Charon pats Joey on the shoulder and leaves.

But with that pat, Charon injects Joey with libericim. The prick in Joey's shoulder is so unnoticeable that Joey doesn't even feel it.

The next morning, Joey is found dead in his cell. And the new guard has disappeared.

Back in the room he has rented, Charon walks around almost in a daze.

He actually feels tears in his eyes. Did he really love Joey after all? But Joey was a risk he couldn't take.

Charon knows that sooner than later Joey would be subjected to a grueling interrogation, perhaps even torture, to give him up.

Charon couldn't take the chance that Joey would break. Joey had to go.

Charon, who had killed more people than he could count, couldn't believe the reaction he is having to Joey's death. Maybe he did love Joey. If so, it's the second one in his entire life that he loved. His little niece was the first.

"That damn priest," Charon utters out loud to himself. "He's gonna pay."

17

George Hamller has asked for an appointment.

I'm sitting waiting for him. His appointment is for 9:30 in the morning. It is now ten minutes to ten.

George is a heavy hitter. He contributes a minor fortune to the parish and all the extra collections.

I'm wondering what's on his mind.

Finally he shows up. No apology for being late. Just walks in and takes a chair. Not even a "Good morning, Father."

Whatever it is, his body language is a message that he is upset about something.

"I am here about the sermon or homily or whatever they're calling it these days which you gave this past Sunday."

Oh, boy, I think to myself, here we go. The homily was on social justice.

13

"Sir," (not Father) I could not disagree more vehemently with you than I am at this moment."

He's a stocky man but not flabby. His steel gray hair has remnants of waves from days gone by. His eyes are piercing blue. His jaw looks like it had been sculpted into his face.

It is obvious that this man is used to dominating, used to throwing his weight around. He is a man of wealth and power. He expects people to agree with him and will brook no resistance.

"In what way or ways do you disagree, Sir?" (One good turn deserves another).

"You quoted some author about our national violence." I reiterate the quotation from Gerard Vanderhaar's book, *Beyond Violence: In the Spirit of the Nonviolent Christ*, "Our national violence is marked by flags, veiled in patriotic oratory, blessed by church officials, upheld by courts, praised by parents, and hailed by historians."

"Yes, yes, that's the one. It may have been a quote, but it was obvious you agreed wholeheartedly with it. Then you went on to quote that Martin Luther King."

Again I repeat. "Martin Luther King called for an end to poverty at home, the reordering of America's values, and a withdrawal from our imperialistic designs around the world."

"Yes, these statements you delivered to a captive audience are nothing but treason. You were attacking our great nation. A nation that offers untold opportunities for ample ..."

"Wealth," I interrupt.

"And power for good throughout the world," he adds. "I pay my dues. I receive Communion every week, I raised my children Catholic. Now you're telling me that I should withdraw my investments in conglomerates because I'm contributing to this social injustice?"

"Not exactly, but that's up to you to decide," I say.

"I'm sick and tired of you people whining about justice, discrimination and slavery centuries ago."

I wince at the slur. "Perhaps you should find another parish," I suggest gently.

"This has been my parish all my life. And I'll still be here long after you're gone which will be soon after I contact the Cardinal. What you glibly call national violence is in fact national security."

It's obvious we're never going to have a meeting of the minds, so I say, "Thank you for taking the time to come and see me. And be sure to give the Cardinal my regards."

He stood up abruptly, threw a hateful stare at me, turned and stomped out.

I have this flashback to the man in the gospel story who decided to build bigger and better barns.

19

My appointment with the Cardinal is for tomorrow at 2 PM.

I suppose he doesn't take an afternoon nap like so many clergy do.

His Eminence seems ambivalent. At one point he says to me that we must always preach social justice. He even quotes Pope Paul VI. "The cry of the poor bars us from making any compromises with any kind of social injustice."

At another point he tells me the we shouldn't clobber (his word) the people with the sledgehammer of our preaching. That just because a man is wealthy doesn't mean he is involved in unjust activities. I wonder if he is worried about losing the thousands Hamller contributes to the diocese, but I don't want to rash judge.

I say, "Your Eminence, the clobbering isn't mine. The clobbering is the way some people perceive and interpret what I am preaching."

It's obvious that nothing beneficial is going to come out of this Kung-fu conversation, so I switch topics to the one I had asked to see the Cardinal about in the first place.

So I tell him about Scuds, Joey and Charon and the threat on my life.

"What do you want to do?" he asks me like an academician quizzing a student about some philosophical theory.

I want to stay exactly where I am," I say to him.

"So be it," the Cardinal ends the conversation except to remind me about clobbering.

I must admit the Cardinal seems disinterested in my bodily welfare. Maybe he thinks I'm too involved in solving crimes. But I don't want to rash judge.

When I get back to the rectory, there's a young man standing by the door. He's wearing a dapper three-piece suit. I can tell from the bulge that he's carrying. He's handsome in a rugged sort of way. Black receding hair, flat brown eyes and a smile that could pick up a hottie in any bar.

"Hello, Father," he says. "My name is Julius Pfeiffer. His Eminence has hired me to watch over you," he says in a quiet, even tone. "Consider me your guardian angel," he smiles angelically.

I thank him and tell him I really don't need him. I tell him to thank the Cardinal for me. He walks away but I suspect he isn't going far.

I think I whisper a prayer that he doesn't.

I smile. The Cardinal's a man of few words but of decisive action. He really does care.

20

Lawrence Oliver Tobin whose initials gained him the nickname, Law and Order Tobin, paces the office with the furor of caged gorilla.

He is a man of medium height. Well-trimmed from working out regularly. His brown hair is messed from running his hand through it habitually. His steel gray eyes search his desk for nothing in particular. His handsome face is screwed up into an impenetrable question mark.

"We had them," he snarls at the small group of the Securities and Exchange Commission agents gathered in his office. Perhaps the cream of the crop among all the agents in the entire Commission.

"With Sterling's testimony we could've got Bradford and Bradford Octogenic Chemicals for corruption, theft, kickbacks, bribery as well as for fraud, market manipulation, blackmail, payoffs, bribery and insider trading."

No one dares to say, "You said bribery twice."

"I want to know who's behind that assassination, who hired this assassin, Charon," Law and Order all but bellowed.

"Easier said than done," one of the agents drawls. "We all know that Bradford and Bradford was behind the murder of Charles Sterling. But which one of the officials of that multinational …? Well, good luck to all of us."

"How certain are we that Charon is the trigger?" another agent asked.

"Who else?" L.O. snapped as he sweeps his arm around the room as though indicating all the possible suspects.

"The police report the telltale chewing gum wrapper. It's Charon all right," one of the men says. "Never any prints," he finishes with a sigh.

"That police report about Charon having that priest in his sights … What's his name? Father Michael or Mike," Law and Order asks.

"That comes from a street bum named Scuds," an agent interrupts. "How reliable is that?"

"It's better than having no lead at all," L.O. whispers as though to tell the others just how desperate he is and they are.

"Look, Pete," L.O. stares intensely at the agent, "find that priest and debrief him. I know he's already talked to the local police, but there may be something more you can discover. You're our best interrogator." L.O. says this to take the sting out of the order.

He knows the agents think this is a waste of time. But he wants any kind of a further lead he could get.

"All right," Pete was obviously annoyed. "But I think a professional hit man like Charon threatening a nobody priest is a waste …"

"Just do it!" L.O. commands.

Pete leaves and the others go back to their desks.

Law and Order Tobin goes into his office, flings his coat over his chair and sits down.

He lets out a heavy sigh. He almost feels like crying. He had had this case wrapped, but now …. Why hadn't he seen the possibility that someone would try to take out his key witness?

21

"Hi, Father Mike," Agent Pete Sokol smiles broadly at me.

"Good afternoon, Agent," I say to him.

"I guess you know why I'm here," the pleasant agent says back to me. "It's about that report about Charon having you in his crosshairs."

I smile to myself at the way the agent tries to use a euphemism to cover up the word assassination.

So I tell him what Scuds told me. I also tell him about the part I played in the capture of Joey Cortello, Charon's "companion," and how the F.B.I. used Joey as bait to get Charon.

Agent Sokol frowns and seems lost in thought.

Then he says, "We got a report earlier today that Joey Cortello was found dead in his cell this morning. Also about a new guard who disappeared after one day on the job."

"Charon?" I ask.

"I had no idea like that till this moment," Sokol says with that light-bulb-over-his-head look.

"I think you had better tell the M.E. to look for some kind of poisonous drug," I say.

"Yesss," the agent says slowly like he can't understand why he didn't think of it.

Then he says, "You're quite the detective, Father. I've heard about you and your deductive powers and your famous intuition.

"Thank you," I respond with a flourish of modesty.

"If they were so close, why would you think Charon would kill Joey?" Agent Sokol asks me.

"Joey's probably the only one who could identify Charon. I would imagine the authorities were just biding their time until they could get Joey to cooperate.

"Makes sense," Sokol says as he looks off as if searching for more questions to apply to my "deductive powers."

Then he says, "That certainly would put Charon here in the vicinity. Near the assassination scene. All we have so far is that chewing gum wrapper. This cements it."

I don't want to rain on his parade by telling him that far from evidence his and my conclusion are only guesswork.

"Well, we still have your safety to be concerned about," Agent Sokol said with warm empathy.

"The Cardinal has procured a guard for me," I tell him, "but I dismissed him."

"Fatalism?" Sokol asks with an arched brow, clearly belying his question.

"God's will," I answer, more like a prayer than a statement of fact.

"By the way," I say, "there's no reason to ask the prison officials for a description. From what I gather, Charon is a master of disguises."

Agent Sokol thanks me for my time and leaves. No doubt he's convinced that Charon is the assassin.

I pray he's not.

22

Stanley Mosley sits behind his huge mahogany desk as though he were perched on a throne.

He's the CEO of Bradford and Bradford Octogenic Chemicals. A bald man with beady eyes in a plump face. Even sitting there it is obvious he is short and bulky. But he exudes power and menace flashes from his every glance.

"Well?" he asks the man standing in front of his desk.

The man is young, full head of black hair combed back with grease. He is handsome but he too gives the impression of being capable of ruthlessness.

"They have no way of tracing it back to us, sir," he responds in a measured tone.

"Sit," Mosley commands.

Robert Bury sits, carefully and a bit hesitantly.

"What makes you sure we're in the clear?" Mosley asks in a grumbling voice. "With this damnable investigation going on, we can't afford to have that nitwit of an assassin hanging around.

"He's a hired assassin. He does his job and leaves."

"What about this threat he's made against the priest? That doesn't sound to me that he's leaving," Mosley's beady eyes narrow.

"I give no credence to that report or more exactly, rumor," Bury replies self-sufficiently. "Why would a professional like Charon want to kill a priest?"

"I understand," Mosley counters, "that this particular priest is a meddler."

"A meddler?" Bury arched a quizzical brow.

"My information, and I might add, information you should have, is that this priest is forever helping the police to solve all kinds of crimes. He's an amateur, but very clever. He's known for his Sherlock Holmes kind of deductive ability."

"If this is true," Mosley continued in a harsh tone, "then you had better make certain that Charon has left the city. Do I make myself clear?"

"Crystal," Bury all but whispers.

Bury gets up and makes a small bow, turns and leaves.

Mosley waves his hand over one of the several phones on his desk.

Quietly he says to the party on the other end, "If Charon is still in the city, exterminate him."

He waves the connection dead, turns to his computizer and begins his day's work.

23

Dr. Jonas Clever, the police psychologist, sits across from Father Mike in the conference room at One Police Plaza.

"How are you feeling, Father?" Clever asks in an almost disinterested way.

I know from previous experience how the good doctor operates. He feigns objectivity in the hope that the "patient" will not feel intruded upon.

"I'm feeling … Well, a bit concerned, a bit frightened, a bit insecure, a bit …"

"I understand," the good doctor cuts Mike off before he's treated to a litany of the priest's emotions. He's sure the priest could go through every possible feeling known to humankind.

"I'm here because of the concern and I'm sure the caring of the Mayor and Chief of Police," Father Mike says. "They apparently want to know how I'm reacting to the possible threat."

Dr. Clever assumes the role of professor so I suppose I'm the student.

"There are four types of assassins," he seems to pontificate.

"One, there is the political type like John Wilkes Booth.

"Then the egomaniac who's looking for some kind of recognition or even notoriety.

"Third, the psychopath who is usually called a 'stone killer,' a cold blooded killer who has no remorse.

"Finally, there is the sufferer from a major mental disorder, frequently delusion."

He takes a breath which gives me an opening.

"There is also a fifth type," I say. "The paid assassin. The one who kills as a way of making a living."

Before the good doctor can respond, I continue.

"Your four types all seem to be psychological misfits. As such they have no *moral* responsibility for their acts of assassination. Frankly, Doctor, I have trouble with your types. I can't see someone taking the life of another not realizing he or she is doing something wrong."

"Ah, Father," the good doctor purred as if he's about to announce 'checkmate,' "there are so many excuses for killing: self defense, warfare, capital punishment. It's difficult to assign your moral responsibility to someone who is psychologically debilitated."

"In my studies," I counter, "I have learned that the first time an assassin kills, he or she suffers tremors, throws up, has sleepless nights. The second time comes easier. By the third murder, the assassin feels nothing. He or she has become your stone killer. It's just too bad that we don't spot the seeds of resentment or hatred before they bloom into the fruit of criminal behavior."

"But the first reaction," I say, "tells me that there is a realization of wrong doing."

"Well," the good doctor says, "this is all theoretical. We have to concentrate on your reaction, your well being."

"In that case, Doctor," I say simply, trying to show gratitude even though the doctor has been ordered to evaluate me, "I am in as good a shape as I can be under the circumstances."

"Do you believe the threat?" the good doctor asked, assuming his detached demeanor.

"I didn't until I heard that Charon's 'companion,' Joey Cortello, died for no apparent reason in prison where a new guard had just been hired and disappeared the day Joey's body was discovered."

"You think this Charon killed this Joey?" the good doctor seemed either intrigued or flabbergasted.

"It makes sense to me," I say. "If Charon is going to stick around to assassinate me or for any other reason, he wouldn't want to take the chance of Joey identifying him.

"Anonymity is his strong suit. That's why he's a master of disguises. But then Joey might know all his disguises. Who knows?"

"It could be as simple or complicated as Charon deciding that if Joey could no longer be his lover he'd be no one's lover in prison."

We sit in silence. I'm not sure what the good doctor is thinking. Finally he says, "Father Mike, I'm convinced you are in danger. Very real danger and I'll report same."

"Whatever," I say. I thank the good doctor and leave. I have hospitals to visit.

24

I sit in my study pondering the good doctor's appraisal of killing – make that murder.

Have we sunk so low in our appreciation of human life that even an esteemed psychologist like Dr. Clever can make excuses for the taking of life.

I am feeling especially unnerved by his example of capital punishment. For me it is the second most barbaric practice of so-called civilized society.

I remember reading somewhere that some spokesperson for the medical community said that a physician could absolutely not be involved in capital punishment according to their code of ethics.

I also remember at the time that physicians could, according to their code, be involved in the murder of pre born children. Something the good doctor didn't mention – abortion, the most barbaric practice.

For now I had to use all my resources to find out where Charon might be.

I start with my "good" friend, Don Giovanni.

I go to Tullio's restaurant where the Don holds court.

Tullio himself comes over. "Hi, Father Mike," he greets me with his usual flourish.

"Hello, Tullio," I say back. "I don't have time for a drink tonight. Is he here?"

"In the back," Tullio answers. "I do think he's expecting you."

"Don Giovanni," I say, "it's good to see you again."

"And you, Father Mike, how goes it with God's business?"

"All's well in that department, Don."

"Ah, but not so well in other areas," he says as he digs deeper into his pasta.

"You still think this Charon is out to ... kill ... you?" He asks with a mouth full of pasta.

"Yes," I say. "But I only have Scuds word on this. The rest is speculation."

"Scuds can be reliable," the Don says and he motions to one of his henchmen to pour him some more wine. He already offered me some wine but I decline.

"So what do you suggest, Don Giovanni?" I ask respectfully.

"I must have time to think about this," he says.

Not much help here, I think but do not say it.

"Thank you for whatever you can do, Don," I say to him as I get up to leave.

"In the meanwhile," the Don says, "I will have some of my boys keep an eye out for you. I would also use that Julius Pfeiffer the Cardinal has sent to you if I were you, Father Mike."

"Good evening, Don Giovanni and may God be with you," I say as I turn and leave, wondering how the Don knows about Pfeiffer.

25

I'm taking the Don's advice seriously.

I'm planning to contact Julius Pfeiffer the guard the Cardinal sent to me.

The problem is I don't know how to contact him.

The problem is resolved almost at once. As I turned the corner, there is Julius.

"Good evening, Father Mike," he says to me as if we are old buddies from high school. "Did you gain any valuable information from Don Giovanni?"

"Only that I should let you watch over me," I say back to him, wondering how Pfeiffer knows I had visited with the Don. What a web we weave.

"Wise advice," Julius says to me.

"What exactly does this entail," I ask with no little annoyance in my voice.

"Just go through your daily routine as you choose to do. I'll be there as a kind of shadow," Julius answers me.

"A shadow won't be much good if Charon shoots me from a sniper's distance as he did with Charles Sterling," I object with what I think is common sense.

"As a shadow," Julius tries to assure me, as we keep walking toward the rectory, "means that I keep an eye out for snipers – and get to them before they can get to you."

"That's a lot for one man," I say to him.

"Father, perhaps I didn't make myself clear enough. The Cardinal didn't hire just me. He hired my entire firm. There will be many who will be looking after your welfare. Many who will be keeping an eye out for a 'sniper.'"

"It seems like a lot of money to throw at my problem, if a problem I have at all," while I'm offering a prayer of thanks for my solicitous Cardinal.

"Oh, Father, you do have a problem. However this Scuds got a hold of this information, I have no doubt that Charon has you in his sights."

There's that "in his sights" again. I wonder if anyone ever says assassination or out to kill you. But I say to him, "Julius, may I call you Julius (he nods), I have to admit that I take Charon's threat seriously. And I feel helpless and very vulnerable. So I appreciate any hovering you and yours can do."

"You have it, Father Mike." With that he shakes my hand and disappears as quickly as he had appeared.

I go to my study upstairs. What seemed at first as a very comfortable living quarters now seemed like a prison.

Could I still go out among my people? Of course I can. If Charon wants to keep me "in his sights," he doesn't have to wait till I leave the rectory and go out in public. He could do it right here in my comfortable quarters.

26

I'm attending this one day workshop for priests on peace and justice.

Although I believe in working for peace and justice and have preached on it often, as George Hamller was quite agitated about that day in my office, but today my mind is far from the topic under discussion.

At a break, I find myself next to Eric Stouffer. Eric had been pastor of a sprawling suburban, quite wealthy, parish. But Eric proved to be more a high powered financier than a loving pastor. Eric is as handsome and suave as a Hollywood idol.

Eric is the type who, as the saying goes, could sell refrigerators to Eskimos.

He has personality rushing out of him like a tumultuous river, sweeping everyone along in his magnetic enthusiasm. If he hadn't been a priest, he would have been a high-powered Vice Chairman in charge of sales in some conglomerate.

The old joke is applied to him. A little boy swallowed a quarter. A neighbor told his parents, "Take him to Father Eric. He can get money out of anybody."

Actually, it isn't a joke. Eric single-handedly raised five point two million for the new priests' retirement home.

He just envelops people, captivates them, schmoozes them.

So the Cardinal makes Eric a Monsignor, relieves him of parish responsibilities so he could be a freelance fund raiser. Something he's doing quite well, even if isn't doing much as a priest. Because of his many talents as a money-raiser, the Cardinal ignores his shortcomings as a priest.

The gold Caddy he drives would be a scandal if any other priest drives it but it is expected of Eric. He easily glad hands the wealthy, powerful and influential.

"Hey, Mike! How's it chugging along?" he asks me with his trademark hail-fellow-well-met verve.

"Fine, Eric," I say back to him. "How's it going with you?"

"Oh, you know. Trying to get that orphanage under way. Still need about three mil."

In his own way, he is helping people: retired priests, orphans. Probably more than I'm doing.

"So, Mike, you're now the pastor of a very plush parish, a lot of heavy hitters."

I take this as a warning that he will be contacting some of those heavy hitters. I hope he stays away from my number one fan, George Hamller.

"What's this I hear that you're under the gun?" (laughs uproariously). "Excuse the pun."

"Nothing to worry about, Eric," I say.

"Good, good," he says, "no one's that interested in you to want to take you out."

I feel the sting of his remark. Yet what he says has some merit. Still I couldn't get Joey's death out of my mind.

Eric drifts off to another group of priests. Actually he glides. He is as smooth as syrup.

27

Charon, the assassin, sits on a park bench watching the children at play in the play ground. Such energy. The children remind him of that battery bunny on TV that keeps going and going.

He wonders what it would be like to have children of his own. To be married and have a family of his own. The momentary ocean wave of enthusiasm turns immediately into a muddy rivulet of despair.

With the sharp edge of realization, he knows he would never know.

Yet again he had millions stashed away. He could leave this life, assume a new identity, move far away, meet someone …

He stops his reverie abruptly. He isn't normal according to the snobbish norms of present day society. He isn't totally heterosexual.

Still he could adopt a child, even children.

But he would have to go through a labyrinth of red tape.

Occupation? Assassin.

Place of residence? The world.

Next of kin? A mother too old to care for herself.

Income? Millions in Swiss banks.

Yes, he would be a prime choice for a foster father or an adoptive father, he thought with cynicism dealing a knock out blow to his dream, his bright hope like a galaxy suddenly becoming a milky blur.

Why is he sitting here? He should have left this city days ago.

But he has one more mission to accomplish.

28

I am sitting in my office. The phone rings.

"Hello, Father Mike.

"Mike, it's Eric.

"Eric?"

"Eric Stouffer."

This is it. Eric's going to ask me about my "heavy hitters." He's going to invade my parish to get donations for whatever he's raising money for this time.

"Mike, I didn't know who to call. I know you get involved in crimes and such. So I thought I'd call you."

"Eric, whatever it is, don't let's talk about it on the phone. Can you come here?"

"I'm being watched. But I can shake them. Can you meet me at … Gromly's, say about three this afternoon?"

I check my calendar. Free all afternoon. "Okay, Eric, Gromly's at three."

It's now twenty after three and no Eric. I'm thinking I'd wait to three thirty then leave.

Suddenly a man approaches my table. He looks as disheveled as a homeless person. But I can tell from his gait that it's Eric.

He sits down, looks around and puts a hand up on his forehead, obviously trying to cover his face.

He looks pitiful. Nothing like the debonair Eric of lore.

"Mike I need your advice. I'm being accused of fraud."

"Fraud?" I ask.

"I bought this relatively large yacht. I did it to have a place to schmooze the heavy hitters."

"A yacht?" I say.

"Granted I used money I collected, but it was to further the cause. Now someone has found out that I used money donated for charity and ..."

Eric pauses letting me fill in the blank.

So I say to him, "And you're being accused of fraud. Who's following you?"

"Some hoodlums. They look really dangerous. I'm out of my league on this one, Mike."

"Can't you just sell the boat and put the money back?" I ask.

"It's not that simple, Mike. My reputation's besmirched. I'll never be able to raise another nickel."

"Can't you come clean. Tell the truth about why you bought the boat?" I ask, trying to arrive at some advice I can give.

"My reputation is ruined, Mike. Hell, I might even be suspended. I'm sure the Cardinal's already heard about it. Maybe he's the one who is sending those hoodlums."

"I doubt it, Eric. But someone is sending them. Eric, you don't need me, you need a lawyer – a really top notch lawyer.

"Of course, I've thought about that. But then it really will be out in the open. My reputation ..."

29

Eric leaves me. I don't give him any worthwhile advice. No advice at all for that matter.

But he doesn't leave before he tells me about the pictures.

He receives the pictures in the mail.

Eric reaches into his coat pocket and pulls out the pictures. He hands them over to me.

They are pictures of him with a very salacious, bikini clad young woman. They are laughing and frolicking and kissing on board his yacht – purchased for schmoozing the filthy rich.

With the pictures is a demand for five million dollars.

Blackmail!!

So it isn't a matter of simple fraud. I don't say that to him.

I do figure that the "hoodlums" following him are just keeping tabs on his whereabouts. They don't pose any danger. No one kills the goose and loses the golden egg. I don't say this to Eric either.

"This is why I can't hire a lawyer," Eric says quite accurately.

I am at a loss. I really don't know what to say.

"This young woman ..." I mange to finally say.

"Just someone I know. Margaret Mosley. Met her at a fund raiser. Well-heeled, spoiled. She wants a permanent relationship. Something, I tell her, I can't give her."

Delving into my proverbial intuition, I ask, "Could she be behind the blackmail? You know, a woman scorned."

"I'm such a fool. A damn fool." Eric begins to sob.

I put my hand on his. Not much of a consolation. Certainly not advice.

I do say to him, "Eric I need time to think this through."

"I know, I know, it's a mess. Mike, I'm done. I don't know what I'm going to do.

But that's not up to me, is it? It's up to the Cardinal."

"Have you been in touch with the Cardinal? I mean on some pretext just to psyche out what his reaction is to you."

"No, right now I think I want to stay as far away from him as possible. All I need to hear is, 'Monsignor, I want to see you ASAP.'"

Eric's right about one thing: it *is* a mess!

Eric doesn't say anything about my intuition about Margaret Mosley.

30

Don Giovanni is more than a little excited.

But he is also engulfed in suspicion.

A Monsignor Bevins calls him and tells him the Cardinal – the Cardinal !! – wants to see him – at his convenience.

That's what the Monsignor says, "at your convenience."

What could the Cardinal – the Cardinal !! – want with him?

To tell him to reform his ways? Threaten him with hell fires? Call him an embarrassment. What could the Cardinal ever want with him?

Well, there is no time like the present.

"Jimmy, bring the car around," the Don orders. "We're gonna see da Cardinal."

On the way, the Don calls Father Mike on his cell phone.

"Hello, Father Mike."

"Hello, Father Mike, dis is Don Giovanni."

"Ah, Don, how are you?"

"Father Mike, the Cardinal wants to see me. I'm on da way now."

"Wow, Don, that's interesting. Did he say what he wanted?"

"Nah, maybe he wants a cut for the diocese." The Don laughs heartily.

"Father Mike, how do I address the Cardinal?"

"Your Eminence would be fine."

"And how should he address me?"

"Don would be appropriate, Don."

31

Monsignor Bevins, the Cardinal's secretary, was taken aback at the sight of Don Giovanni. Or perhaps it was his three "bodyguards" that wrenched his gut.

"I'm Don Giovanni. I'm here to see da Cardinal."

The Don hardly gave any sign of recognition to the young priest. As though he were a bug on the windshield of life.

This annoyed Bevins no end. "You should have called ahead and made an appointment," Bevins does his best to appear as haughty as possible.

"Look, Buddy," one of the Don's henchmen sounded as ominous as threatening earthquake, "da Cardinal invited the Don here to come here. So here he is."

Just then the office door opened and the Cardinal appeared.

"That's fine, Monsignor, the Don doesn't need an appointment. I've cleared my calendar for him."

Don Giovanni huffs and expands his broad chest as if he were a rooster trotting around the chicken yard.

"Youse wait here," he says to his men. "Keep pretty boy here company while me and da Cardinal talks business."

"Please, Don Giovanni, have a seat," the Cardinal points to a couch while he sits in a chair off to the right of the couch.

"Thanks, yur Eminence," the Don pronounces the title most accurately.

The Cardinal nods approval of the Don's using a respectful title.

"Let me get right down to it, Don," the Cardinal says most seriously, as he pulls his chair a little closer. The Don leans forward all ears.

"You know Father Mike very well?" the Cardinal asks rhetorically.

"Yeah, Eminence, I know him real well. A hell … heck of a man. True blue. Very respectful. A good detective too."

"You also know there's a threat on his life?" Again rhetorical.

"So he tells me. Dis assassin Charon."

"Have you been able to give him any help in this matter?" Not rhetorical.

"I'm afraid not, Eminence."

They both sit in silence for a few moments.

Then the Cardinal: "Don Giovanni, I am aware of the many resources you have at your disposal. This assassin is inhuman. Ridding the world of him would be a great service to humankind."

Don Giovanni looks a bit startled. The Cardinal is asking him to take out Charon.

"Can you do anything along these lines?" the Cardinal asks knowing that the Don clearly gets his message.

"It might be difficult, Eminence. This Charon is a shadow. And nobody knows what he looks like. I can see what can be done. But I can't promise nothin.'"

"Anything you can do. I treasure Father Mike as you do," the Cardinal speaks persuasively, with his hands clasped as if he were praying.

The Don was visibly impressed with a Cardinal of the Church asking for a favor and what a favor.

"I want to protect Father Mike in whatever way I can, Eminence."

"This assassin has to be, how would you put it, neutralized," the Cardinal's voice was almost conspiratorial.

"That's a good word, Eminence. Neutralized. I'll see what I can do. You have my word on that.

With that the Cardinal rises and extends his hand. Don Giovanni shakes it firmly and turns to leave.

As the Don reaches the door, he turns. "And here I thought you was gonna ask me for something simple like half of my take for the diocese." The Don chuckles.

The Cardinal throws back his head and lets out a loud laugh.

"God bless and keep you, Don Giovanni."

32

I am circling around. I have Miss Mosley's address.

I drive up the circular driveway to the mansion.

I ring the door bell. A butler answers.

"Hello," I say to the butler. I'm here to see Miss Margaret Mosley."

"Do you have an appointment, sir?" The butler is obviously officious and enjoys being so.

"No, I don't. I didn't know I had to have an appointment."

"Sorry, sir, you'll have to have an appointment."

"Who is it, Herman?" a voice from behind the butler asks.

"A gentleman to see you, m'am, but he doesn't have an appointment."

"I'll see him," she says as she peers out at me, decked out in my Roman collar.

"As you wish, Miss Margaret."

Miss Margaret is indeed a beautiful young woman. She's stands at about five foot ten. Glistening blond hair, falling freely down to her shoulders. Bright blue eyes and full lips that seem to invite kisses. A voluptuous figure to say the least. I can easily see why Eric is attracted to her. She is a prize. Under other circumstance, a "keeper."

"Who are you?" she asks me, as if letting me know that I don't have an appointment.

"I'm Father Mike."

"And what do want to see me about?"

"May I come in?"

"Okay, I guess, but I don't know what it is you want to see me about?"

She is patently nervous. I think she knows quite well that this is about Eric.

We stand in the foyer. She makes no move to invite into a sitting room of which I'm sure there are plenty.

So I plunge right in. "I'm here about Monsignor Eric Stouffer. I ..."

"What's between me and Eric is our business," she interrupts petulantly.

"That's not exactly accurate. You and Eric have been photographed in compromising situations which has been brought to the Cardinal's attention," I white lie. Or maybe it has been brought to his attention for all Eric and I know.

"So what does the Cardinal have to do with me and Eric?" Her defenses are up like an high electric fence and ready to fry anyone who comes near.

Eric did say she was spoiled. And she certainly proving that to be true.

I calculate that she's in her late twenties or early thirties, but she reacts like a thirteen year old.

"Do you know that someone is trying to blackmail Eric with those photos?" I persist.

"Blackmail?" she whines in a little voice.

"Blackmail," I reply firmly, hoping that maybe I can intimidate her and knock down some of her electric fences.

"Both Eric and I are wondering who would be doing the blackmailing," I say.

"I don't like your tone," she snaps back at me. "Are you trying to implicate me in blackmailing Eric?"

She is bright.

Before I can answer, she says, "I love Eric. I want to marry him," she almost screeches.

"But," I retort, "he has told you that marriage is out of the question."

"He said he'd think about it. He could join my father's conglomerate and with his talents, he could be making seven figures in no time. We could live very comfortably."

I figure she means live in the way I'm accustomed to.

So I say to her, "If Eric would decide to remain a priest, blackmailing him might be a defiant thrust to force him to reconsider."

There I say what I want to say to her. Now I wait for her reaction.

"You're insane." This time she screams at me. "You dolt. I can have any man of my choosing. I don't have to blackmail anyone into marrying me."

"Thank you for your time, especially seeing me without an appointment."

I leave but I'm still not convinced that Miss Margaret Mosley is not behind the blackmail.

She is a young woman who gets what she wants, by whatever means.

I hope I'm not rash judging her.

33

Driving home, I am still feeling Miss Margaret's sting.

As I am leaving she says, as she spots the two men in the car behind my car, "You must think you're really important. Two bodyguards!"

I must give Julius Pfeiffer and his firm due credit. The Cardinal knew who he was hiring to protect me.

Pfeiffer and his men follow me everywhere except to the bathroom and the confessional. Even then they are only a few steps away.

I must treat them to Chinese one of these days.

Yet I don't feel all that secure. Charon can pick me off with a long range riffle any time he chooses, no matter how many guards there are.

I have to give Eric credit, I'm thinking.

Miss Margaret is a beauty, even if she leads an absolutely pampered life.

I'm praying that if or when the Cardinal confronts Eric, he'll realize how dedicated to his priesthood he is.

I'm not sure if I were in Eric's position I could be as adamant about staying in the active ministry.

But then I am not Eric: handsome, smooth, witty, magnetic. So I would never get into the situation Eric's in.

Still, as I reflect, there's something deeper than Eric's flamboyance. Despite what is probably his infatuation with Miss Margaret, he has a profound loyalty to his priesthood.

More so than many.

I don't believe Miss Margaret's telling me Eric said he'd think it over.

Although joining the 'conglomerate' is more tempting than Miss Margaret.

Infatuations disappear like a wisp of smoke, but job security remains forever, especially a job that garners 'seven figures.'

Eric's in a bind. He's being tortured. I must get back to him.

Miss Margaret has probably already called him to tell him about the intrusive priest.

Sometimes I wonder why I can't just mind my own business. I hope it's because of my concern.

I remember reading somewhere that Father Hesburg, the former President of Notre Dame, called a student in to confront him about his immoral behavior. The student said, "It's none of your business." To which Hesburg replied, "It may not be any of my business but it certainly is part of my concern."

I'll have to think about some way to help Eric out of his quagmire.

Eric may be a non conformist but he's not a maverick.

I have to pray fervently for guidance, even illumination.

34

The phone rings at about eleven at night.

"Father Mike," I say into the receiver.

"Father Mike, it's me, Christine Joyce ..."

"Christine!" I exclaim. "It's so good to hear from you." She's doing such a wonderful job managing Forrow Haven.

"I hope it's not too late."

"Christine, you know you can call me any time of the day and night. What's up?"

"I'm afraid it's bad news."

I freeze, feeling ice shooting up and down my spine. A premonition. I don't know if I can handle any mashing and mangling announcement. My joy at hearing Christine's voice hisses like a pricked balloon.

"What is it, Christine?" I ask, feeling myself plunging into insulating despair.

"Another girl has been murdered. Oh, Father Mike!" Christine breaks down into tumultuous tears, floodwaters of consternation and helplessness.

"No ..." I stifle my disbelief even though I had an intuition as to what the bad news might be.

"Christine, is anyone with you? Do you want me to come over?"

"No, no, you don't have to come over. It's too late. The girls are here with me, but they're more upset than I am."

"Look, Christine, forget the time. I'll be right over."

I can't be a chance bystander. Someone written out of the script of life, no matter how despicable the events that assail us – me.

35

By the time I reach Forrow Haven, Detective Alison Masconi is already there.

"Hello, Father Mike," she said more pleasantly than circumstances warranted.

"Detective," I said rather somberly.

I hug Christine. She is sobbing. I try to console her but to no avail.

I disengage myself and turn to Detective Masconi. "Detective?" I indicate I'm looking for information on the murder.

Christine speaks up. "It's Sally. She went out about nine. I waited for her to come home. She didn't." Christine is weeping again.

"The girls and I thought she might have slipped back into her old profession. So we went out looking for her.

"We found her two blocks down from the Haven, lying on the sidewalk."

"Detective Masconi broke in. "Her head was crushed in. It's like before ..."

I am back to my original fear. Did Jim get away? Was he back on the street, killing prostitutes?

I turn and pick up the phone. I call the sanatorium.

"Yes," the voice responded.

"St. Luke's?" I ask.

"Yes," came the answer. Why wouldn't she announce that it is St. Luke's when she answers. Who knows the nebulous vagaries of telephone operators?

"Will you please check to see if Father James Norwood is in his room?" trying to hide my annoyance with her.

"I'll connect you with our night supervisor," she replied officiously.

"Yes, what can I do for you?" The voice was one used to issuing commands and putting up with no nonsense.

I identify myself and repeat my request.

"I can't do that," she answered authoritatively.

"Look," I say, letting all my frustration pour into my voice, "this is a matter of life and death. Your superior will be very interested in your refusal to fulfill the Cardinal's request."

One of these days, the Cardinal is going to find out how I throw his authority around and I'll take another plunge into his hot water. He's already told me that I do not speak for him. He has a PR priest to do that.

The supervisor apparently is intimidated. "I'll check," she said.

"Father Norwood is in his room, tucked in for the night, enjoying his perpetual coma." She sounds as contemptuous as a drum major reaming out a marcher for being out of step.

"Thank you," I say politely and the Cardinal thanks you too. In for one, in for two.

"Thank God," I breathe a sincere prayer.

36

I reach into my intuition. "Ladies," I said respectfully, "I think we can deduce that Sally went back to her profession. And a John for whatever reason assaulted her."

They don't look convinced. So I suggest that we all go into the chapel and offer a prayer for Sally.

Once we are settled, I read part of a Chapter from Matthew's gospel: The women are shaken and worried.

"Therefore I tell you, do not be anxious about your life, what you shall eat or what you shall drink, nor about your body, what you shall put on. Is not life more than food, and the body more than clothing? Look at the birds of the air: they neither sow nor reap nor gather into barns, and yet your heavenly Father feeds them. Are you not of more value than they? And which of you by being anxious can add one cubit to his span of life? Are you anxious about clothing? Consider the lilies of the field, how they grow; they neither toil nor spin; yet I tell you, even Solomon in all his glory was not arrayed like one of these. But if God so clothes the grass of the field, which today is alive and tomorrow is thrown into the oven, will he not much more clothe you, O men of little faith? Therefore do not be anxious, saying, 'What shall we eat?' or 'What shall we drink?' or 'What shall we wear?' For the Gentiles seek all these things; and your heavenly Father knows that you need them all. But seek first his kingdom and his righteousness, and all these things shall be yours as well. Therefore do not be anxious about tomorrow, for tomorrow will be anxious for itself. Let the day's own trouble be sufficient for the day."

Then I offer a prayer for Sally and for all of us asking God to give us strength and courage.

It wasn't much but I think the woman felt a bit better. Some thank me and others even ask me to keep them in my prayers.

Christine and I go into her office.

"You're going to have your hands full," I say to Christine.

"They're filled every day."

"Is it becoming too much?" I ask gently.

"Some days are more difficult than others. Then I think of my sister giving her life and I ask myself, 'Can I do less?'"

I reach over and hold her hand. "You are a wonderful person, Christine. I admire you more than I can express."

"Thank you, Father Mike, and thanks for coming over.

I leave Christine's office to face Detective Masconi.

"Are you serious about the John?" she asks in a non confrontational tone. "Or are you just trying to settle the girls down?"

"I am serious. Once I found out that Jim is snug in his bed, I have this hunch that what I said to them is true."

"I guess so," Alison sighs. She too has her hands full.

I guess we all do, what with an assassin hanging over my head or more precisely behind my back.

Oh well, God's will be done.

Suddenly there was a screech. Christine rushes from her office. "One of the girls is having a meltdown," she shouts.

But it isn't a meltdown. There is a huge man coming down the corridor, flailing a knife.

Alison Masconi draws her gun. "Stop or I'll shoot," she yells at him. But he picks up his pace, heading right for us, knife now uplifted.

Masconi shoots him. He twists and falls flat on his face.

My two guardians whom I tell to go into the kitchen and get a cup of coffee, come rushing out. But it is all over like a streak of lightning.

Masconi calls precinct headquarters. Then she stoops down. "He's dead," she says as matter of factly as if saying the coffee's ready. She searches his pockets looking for some identification.

"Look at this," she says, holding up an thin gold necklace.

"That's Sally's," Christine shouts. "That's Sally's."

"Well," Alison says, "that murder is solved." Again totally emotionless.

I look away. I feel myself trembling at the sight of a man shot to death, bringing up my own fear like the burst of a geyser.

I only hope and pray that these other women would learn a lesson that is taught tonight the hard way.

I don't know if I will sleep peacefully or restlessly tonight.

37

I am on my way home from an early morning sick call.

As I come to the rectory door, someone steps out of the shadows.

An earthquake of a shudder smashes through my entire body.

And my intuition isn't anymore off the mark than an arrow hitting a bull's eye.

"Charon?" I ask trying not to sound plaintive.

"The same, priest," he says sounding as foreboding as an ominous fortune teller.

"And you're here to kill me?" I ask in as a matter-of-fact tone I could muster.

"Not now, now yet, priest." He now sounds as tranquil as a gentleman at a tea party.

"Then…?" I ask.

"I just want to see what kind of a jerk would put my friend in jail."

"I didn't. The police did." Then I worry that I might have implicated the police and made them targets of this mad man.

"You were there. In the church. They used your church."

Just then my two body guards emerge from the dark. Both holding guns. In a threatening voice one of them said, "On the ground, Charon, hands behind your head."

In a circling move as fast as a sleek panther, Charon swings around and shoots both guards dead. Then in another swift move, he lunges into the bushes and disappears.

I stand there shaking uncontrollably like a thin branch in a whirlwind.

Finally, in the rectory, I manage to take out my cell phone. First, I call Detective Masconi and tell her what just happened. She says she'll be right over and not to touch anything.

Next I call Julius Pfeiffer. This is a much more difficult call since I have to tell him that two of his men are dead. This may be enough to make him haul his guards away.

Alison Masconi arrives first. "They're both dead," she said in that same fatalistic tone she uses, I suppose, at all murder scenes. "Yes," I say. I'm still feeling like my stomach is ready to explode.

Next Julius shows up. "How did it happen?" he asks totally exasperated.

"I don't know," I say. "He … Charon … just swung around and fired. It was so fast I couldn't believe it was happening."

"They're two of my best men," Julius sighs heavily.

"They had the drop on him," I say, then I realize I wasn't exactly making them out to be two of the best and I feel embarrassed. My embarrassment is a welcome change from the riotous fear I am feeling.

"How are you doing, Father Mike?" Julius asks.

Finally someone is caring about me. "I'm very shaken," I reply rather sheepishly.

"I'm not at all surprised," Detective Masconi says with what sounds like empathy.

"Tell me, Father," Julius says, "did you get a look at Charon?"

"It was dark. I think I got a glimpse. He …"

"Good enough, Father," Detective Masconi sounds excited. "If you don't mind – and I know what you've been through – come with me to Detective Masconi's station while that 'glimpse' is still fresh in your memory. We'll do an imaging."

"I'll have four of my men here within minutes to go with you, Father," Julius says as sincerely as if he were telling me he is sorry for all his sins.

38

"How's it look?" Detective Paul Morissey asks.

"Not great," the agent in charge of imaging says back to him.

"Yeah, but it's still more than we had, right?" Morissey says.

I am feeling rather useless. With all my powers of observation, I fail in this most crucial test.

"What about the rest of him, Father?" Morissey asks.

Now here is where I can hit at least a single.

"He stands about six feet four or five. He's huge. Very broad shoulders. Barrel chest. He's strong. Big and strong."

"That's something," Morissey's being very cooperative and even complimentary.

"As big as he is," I say, "his moves are as lithesome as a jungle cat."

"The bigger they are, the harder they fall," the imaging agent smirked.

"As the saying goes," I say, "I don't want to rain on your parade, but Charon is a master of disguises. For all we know he was wearing a disguise when I encountered him."

A drab silence envelops the room in the aftermath of the cherry bomb revelation I had just made, snapping the enthusiasm like a breaking twig.

"Well," Detective Morissey says, "this is all we have. Get it out. Who knows …?"

I can tell from his hesitancy that his previous self-assurance has evaporated like fog in an early morning sunshine.

39

I go back to the rectory.

My body guards are really cramping me. I feel the vertigo of dependency.

One in front, one behind and two on either side.

I'm wondering how the Cardinal is paying for this. I should care. Yes, I guess I really should care.

Now Charon knows that I am being protected. I'm wondering if this makes a difference to him. Or is this just another challenge for him to fit the pieces into the jig- saw puzzle.

I can't help being obsessed with this threat to my life as if it were the four walls of paranoia closing in on me.

I can't help wondering why God would want to call me at this point in my life. I feel I have so much more to do.

There are people in my new parish who are in such desperate need. And many of them don't even know it.

People who are convinced that all they have to do is fulfill their religious obligations without giving a thought to the need to clean up the psychological garbage that is cluttering their lives.

People who can be so pious yet their religiosity is a cover up for some deep unadmitted emotional problem.

I suppose all I can do is be resigned to God's plan for me. Resignation is not fatalism.

I know full well that fatalism is the conviction that nothing can be done. That I cannot change anything. That there is no hope.

This cannot be my attitude. While I still have the breath of life, I will do whatever it takes to bring down this psychotic assassin. Especially before he brings me down into my grave.

To ignore or avoid my responsibility is nothing more than neurotic fatalism.

I must do all I can to rid the world of Charon before I reach out to resignation.

I remember reading somewhere that resignation is stoicism, but initiative is Christian.

I'm thinking now about how I can take the initiative. How I can strike first before Charon strikes out at me.

I haven't a single idea.

47

It's come sooner than I expect.

Monsignor Eric Stouffer comes by to see me.

My four body guards have set up their station in the living room, leaving Eric and me alone to talk.

"Mike, my world's caving in," he says. I can almost hear the tears in his voice.

"Eric," what does the Cardinal expect of you?" I ask.

"Well, he didn't suspend me. That's a plus. It's the only one."

"What then?" I ask again.

"I'm to resign my position as fund raiser. He's appointing me pastor of some little parish in Nowheresville. I'm not to introduce any new fund raising in the parish. Oh, and I'm to turn over a total sheet on the funds I've raised and all the money I have garnered."

"It's not all that bad compared to what it could have been," I say, hoping to sound encouraging.

"Did he ask you about the girl?" I know I'm launching out into the deep here, but Eric came to me.

"Oh yeah. I'm not allowed to make contact or see her ever. He even asked me if I wanted to leave and marry her. I said, 'Hell no!'"

Once again I admire Eric's loyalty. I just hope she's not behind the pictures and will publish them.

So I ask, "What about the pictures?"

"Who cares now?" It's the first time Eric seems aggressive. "I'm so ruined that one more blast won't sink me. The Cardinal and I covered this totally. He really grilled me about her. Asked me very personal questions about our relationship. I was open and honest. That's probably why he asked me if I wanted to leave."

"Eric," I say, "I can only repeat that what the Cardinal meted out to you is far less than what he could have. He didn't even take away your honor as Monsignor which in itself is still a sign of his esteem for the work you've done."

"Yeah, I guess so," but he didn't sound convinced.

Probably Eric was just too concerned about his career which has just plunged like the inevitable trajectory of a meteor as far down as possible, at least from his point of view.

With a heavy sigh, Eric gets up. His drink still untouched. "Thanks, Mike," he said simply.

I walk him to the front door. My body guards get up and come around me as I open the door.

Eric heads out into the dark, moonless night. Suddenly there is the sound of a shot and Eric falls backwards onto the ground. Eric is wearing his black clerics.

The body guards pull me back inside. They peer out through the open door. They don't move out. No doubt for fear the sniper or assassin is still there.

One of the men, Paul by name, calls for backup and tells whoever about the sniper outside the rectory.

Eventually, with the backup in place, two of the body guards venture out.

"He's dead," one calls back.

My stomach does a figure eight. "My God," I moan. Then, body guards or not, I rush out, kneel down beside Eric's body and extend absolution. Tears flood my eyes and before I realize it, I'm crying unabashedly.

One of the guards comes over to me and helps me up. "Let's get inside, Father," he says gently and helps me back into the rectory.

"Father Mike, the other guard says, "it's Charon. They found the telltale chewing gum wrapper near where he must have been perched."

I know I'll never forget the sound of the siren as the ambulance takes Eric off into the night.

41

This time the Cardinal doesn't summon me to his inner sanctum.

He comes to my place. No fanfare. Not even Monsignor Bevins. Just the Cardinal as plain and simple as a priest next door. He even drove himself. I'm surprised he still knows how.

"Mike," he says as he embraces me. The very first time. It was like a shockwave that cracked the smooth surface of my composure.

My eyes filled. All I could say, as though I were a mute, was, "Eric."

"Come, sit down, Mike," the Cardinal invited as gently as a doting grandfather.

I walk slowly into the living room and sit down, rather collapse, in a chair. I'm dead tired, not having got any sleep the night before.

The Cardinal sits down across from me.

"I'm so sorry about Eric. I'm sorry our relationship ended on such a sour note. It is one of the most difficult things I had to do, believe me. Eric was the consummate fund raiser. But most of all he was dedicated to his priesthood. That is as obvious as his handsome looks. It's just so, so terrible."

"Frankly," I say, "I feel like hell. He dies because the assassin mistook him for me. I will never get over it. Never!"

"Mike, we have to do something. Make an important decision. It's clear that this assassin is determined to kill you. Poor Eric. The fact that the assassin mistook him for you is proof enough."

"What do you suggest, Cardinal?" I ask without much interest in his response.

"We've got to move you away from here."

This peaked my interest. as if he had just poked me with an elbow.

"If, as you say, Cardinal, he's determined to kill me, where can I go where he can't find me?"

"Mike, I treasure you. I don't want what happened to Eric to happen to you."

"Again, where can I go?" I ask stubbornly.

"I don't know. Somewhere far from here. You could go to another diocese. I would give you a sterling commendation." The Cardinal's just as stubborn.

"He'll find me. Charon's obsessed. He holds me responsible for taking his lover away from him. He said so." It's not easy debating with your Cardinal.

So I take the leap. "Are you placing me under obedience, Your Eminence?" I use his title to give the impression of submission. Cardinals like that.

"No, I wouldn't command you to leave. I just don't want you shot down." He sighs audibly. I win.

"So I'll stay here. Maybe I can track Charon down. I do have a talent along those lines.

"I hope your people are prepared for the shock of your death." The Cardinal's already written me off. Maybe he's right. I don't know. I guess I'll just have to trust in God's loving Providence.

I have a lot to pray over.

42

Margaret Mosley's screams are like a sharp steel spike. Then she screeches like a whining siren. She could be heard all over the house.

She had just seen the televised report on the shooting death of Monsignor Eric Stouffer outside St. Ignatius' rectory.

She throws artifacts against the wall, tries to smash furniture and is just one huge chaotic turbulence.

Her maid tries to calm her but it's as useless as trying to squeeze toothpaste back into the tube.

She is ranting and raving uncontrollably, inconsolable to the point of being suicidal or so it seems to her maid.

"NO! NO! NO!" she keeps screaming repeatedly like a metronome gone wild.

The report stated that the suspect is a professional assassin by the name of Charon.

Exhausted she slumps into a chair, waves her maid away, puts her head in her hands and sobs viciously.

Her father Stanley Mosley, CEO of Bradford and Bradford Octogenic Chemicals, hears his daughter's outburst, but makes no move to go to her. Over the trying years he's grown used to her childish tantrums.

Suddenly, with the rage of a pit bull, she jumps up and rushes to her father's study.

"You rotten, lousy bastard!" she screams at him.

Her father barely glances up at her. Over the trying years he's grown used to her abuse.

"You brought that maniac assassin to this city!" she bellows.

Her father looks up and serenely says, "I beg your pardon."

"You think I don't know what you do. Your secret huddles here in your office. Your surreptitious phone calls. Your plotting, scheming, conspiring. You think I don't know about your maneuver to get rid of Charles Sterling because he was going to sell you out?"

In a voice as calm as if he were describing a rare painting, her father says, "I don't have the slightest idea what you are screaming about." He emphasizes the word screaming for effect.

It has no impact on Margaret. Now she is seething.

"That scumbag you hired has taken away the only man I've ever loved. You had him kill Eric, didn't you?

"Don't be ridiculous," Stanley Mosley replies in a somber, measured tone. "I couldn't care less as to whom your new fling is with."

"But the fact that you brought that assassin here resulted in Eric's murder," Margaret screeches.

"Margaret, please," her father said in a continuing solemn, tired tone, "you're obviously upset. Plan a trip. Go somewhere to relax. And stop bothering me with your tirade."

Margaret pivots and stomps out of the study. A huff would be a monumental understatement. It's an explosion.

Stanley Mosley picks up the phone. "My daughter knows about Charon *and* Sterling."

43

Now I am faced with another problem.

My parochial vicar, Father Kurt Lambose, a convert from Episcopalianism, contacts Monsignor Bevins, the Cardinal's insufferable secretary, and asks for a transfer.

He's not a young man. He's heavyset, bald and his face is scarred with the remnants of acne. He is not attractive physically.

But worse, he has brought a lot of his personal baggage to the priesthood.

I remember one time listening to his homily.

He said, "Two men were driving to confession. One was really sorry for his sins, the other wasn't. They both were in car accidents and were killed. Which one went to heaven?" He answered, "Neither one because they both broke the law."

Needless to say, there is an tumultuous uproar from the congregants who apparently know more theology than Father Lambose.

I call Kurt into my office.

"Kurt," I say to him, "what in the world were you thinking when you made that statement?"

He refuses to answer. But I could sense his anger at being confronted.

"The Church itself," I say, "has never said anyone is in hell. The message you delivered is that confession is the only way to have sins forgiven. There is more to sin and forgiveness than breaking the law. What about the infinite mercy of God?"

Again he does not respond. Nor would he sit down. He just stands there clenching his fists. Obviously he doesn't think he should be questioned.

So I continue, "There are theologians who advance the idea that God has already forgiven us every evil we *will* ever do. He does not even wait for us to commit a sin. His forgiveness has already been given to us provided we repent. They don't say anything about going to confession. They talk about repentance."

"Are you finished?" he asks arrogantly.

"No," I say, "from now on you will submit your homilies to me before you preach them."

With that he makes an about face and stalks out of my office.

He doesn't consult with me about leaving St. Ignatius. After his transfer comes in, he tells me that he isn't going to stay around here and get shot in my place like Monsignor Stouffer did. More arrogance.

Then he adds, "You are the heretic not me."

With that he picks up his bags and leaves.

44

Kurt's replacement is Ambrose Hecken.

Ambrose, whose nickname is Skip, is a big, burley man, robust with a deep and loud laugh.

He's a former Army chaplain who has two Purple Hearts to his credit.

He won one of those Purple Hearts when he pulled a pilot out of a burning plane and got wounded himself in saving the life of that pilot.

Nothing seems to faze him -- not even the threat to my life, then why should it? It's my life!

But to his credit, he tells me not to worry. As long as he's here, I'm safe.

Certainly a God-send.

Ambrose is gentle with the people and loves the little children in our school. They return his love unconditionally.

His homilies are upbeat. He says to me, "These people come here on the weekend after a week of stress and turmoil. They're looking for a reason to go back into the next week with some hope."

How refreshing after the browbeating they took from his predecessor.

Ambrose asks me about the whole situation with the assassin. He has heard about it but wants me to tell him in detail which I do.

Ambrose gets up from the table, goes to room and comes back with a revolver in hand. It's a Magnum .357.

"I have a license for this," he says. "And I know how to use it."

As comforting it is, I doubt if his Magnum would be of any use against the sniper rifle of Charon.

Still it is a reassurance to have Ambrose around. If nothing else, he distracts me with his war stories and his contagious laughter.

I need to thank God for small, no, make that great favors.

45

Problems seem to be pouring in on my like someone blew up a dam.

But they serve to keep my mind busy.

This one is a visit from J. D. Trotter.

"Hello, Father Mike," she says purring. "Thank you for seeing me. I'm J. D. Trotter, the novelist. Perhaps you've read some of my novels.

"Yes," I say, "I've read quite a few."

"What do you think of them?" Still purring.

"Want an honest answer or just flattery?" I ask honestly.

"Why, the honest answer, of course." No purring.

"Well," I say in a straight forward manner, "I think the novels I read are contrived.

"Contrived?" Now absolutely no purring, rather edgy.

"Yes," I say, "the plots are, well, transparent."

"Transparent?" Now haughty.

"Well, it may be due to my predilection to crime solving, but I always find that I figure out your conclusion beforehand.

"Well ..." she's speechless. She asks me to be honest, but when I am ...

"May I ask why you wanted to see me?" I ask.

"You yourself alluded to it. Your predilection to crime solving."

"And you want to talk to me about this because ..."

"To be frank," she undoubtedly is picking me up on my being frank with her, "I'm going to include your character – not your name" she's smug, "in my next novel."

"And you want my permission?"

"I don't need your permission," she says, haughty again. "It's a work of fiction. What I want is some insight into your crime solving ability."

"There's really nothing to it," I say, "I just follow the clues and with a bit of intuition, I come to conclusions. Sometimes on target, sometimes not."

"You were certainly on target when you turned in one of your own. That Father Jim Norwood ..."

"That's a very, very sad episode in my life. I don't want to talk about it."

"Certainly you must have some feelings you haven't shared."

"Feelings I'm not going to share," I say stubbornly.

"How do you feel about being the target, to use your word, of an assassin's bullet?" She really is impertinent.

"How would you feel?" I counter. Then, "I'm frightened. Desperately frightened."

"It must have been quite the ordeal when another priest was killed in your place?"

"Miss Trotter, you seem to have a handle on the facts of my life. Surely, in a work of fiction, you can supply the emotions."

With that I bring the tête-à-tête to a close. "Good afternoon, Miss Trotter," I say with a sufficient amount of abruptness. "Good luck on your next novel."

"I'll try not to make it transparent," she says as haughtily as she could. With that she leaves.

46

Detective Alison Masconi pays a visit.

"Father Mike, I can't tell you how sorry I am about your friend."

"Thank you, Alison," I say. I don't know which is more a burden, the loss of Eric or the solicitude being shown to me because of his murder.

"No doubt," Alison says, "this is the work of Charon. "He's really out to get you. Now he'll be so frustrated he'll be furious."

"Good," I say.

"Good?"

"If he's furious he'll make mistakes. That is out of character for him. He'll do something stupid, maybe show himself."

"That's a stretch, Father." She isn't convinced. But I'm certain of my intuition. One thing I know is the criminal mind.

"What are you going to do, Father Mike? Just sit here like a clay pigeon?"

"Clay pigeons are on the move, Alison. What I'm going to do right now is find out who hired Charon."

"How are you going to do that?"

"Visit Bradford," I say simply like I'm telling her the porch light's on.

"They've already been 'visited' and nothing. If they're responsible for Sterling's murder, there's no way we can pin it on them."

"I'm pretty good at reading body language," I say without no flourish of pride.

"Who is it you're going to see?" Alison asks with no enthusiasm.

"I'm going to the top. Stanley Mosley is the CEO. Him."

"And what do you expect? 'Yes, Father Mike, I hired an assassin to kill Charles Sterling.'"

"Not quite, but I'd like to see him squirm. No matter how much of a rock they like to think they are, if they have something to hide, they squirm."

"You're something else, Mike." It is the first time she smiles. The first time she addresses me informally, using my name without the title. It's amazing how people think that Father is our first name.

47

I am ushered into the office of Stanley Mosley which is as ornate and luxurious as a palace. I am surprised that I get in so easily. My expectation is that I would be kept waiting until the final angel blew eternal horn on the end of time and creation.

Although I get in rather rapidly, Mr. Mosley is about as congenial as a poisonous snake. He finds no trouble letting me know I'm interfering with his very busy day like a brown-out in his highly lit office.

In contrast to his multi thousand dollar suit, I feel shabby. I am trying to control my overloaded nervous system. Especially when I intend to confront this man of a power that screams off the electronic scanner.

Stanley Mosley is an icy fortress of a man with eyes as hard, sharp and black as a hewed edge of a stone that scans you under the edge of emotion. No father of a prodigal son or daughter in his case.

"Thank you for seeing me, Mr. Mosley," I say politely. Men of power like politeness.

"What can I do for you, sir?" he asks without looking up from the paper he's holding in his hand as indifferent as a mannequin, his breathing like the slow switch of a rattlesnake's tail.

"I've had the pleasure of meeting your daughter, Margaret," I say, again as politely as a butler.

"Pleasure?" This time a smile or rather a sinister scowl crosses his lips.

"Somewhat," I say as pleasantly as a congenial bartender.

"What is it you want to see me about?" he asks abruptly like someone who deals thoroughly with the bottom line.

"To be frank," I say, feeling more than tentative, "I want to talk to you about the murder of Charles Sterling ..."

"What does that have to do with you?" he interrupts. "Besides, I've answered all the questions concerning that matter to the local police and the FBI."

Here I go, I think to myself. "I'm curious as to who would have brought in a professional assassin to ..."

"We don't know that," he says brusquely.

"I couldn't notice that you referred to the murder" – I keep repeating this word – "as 'that matter.' It seems to me that you would have referred to Charles Sterling by name."

"That's because you are a priest or whatever. I have no time for sentimentality. Sterling was just another cog in the wheel."

This guy is good. Total ice. Perhaps that's how you get ahead in their world.

"But," I retort, "he was a cog that was going to bring the wheel to a grinding halt if not wreck it completely."

"So I've heard." Talk about being haughty. He's totally stone-hearted.

"So," I persist, "if he was going to blow the whistle, that would be reason enough to have him silenced – permanently."

"What exactly are you getting out, sir?"

"Look Mr. Mosley," I say very openly, "this assassin has threatened my life and has murdered a very dear friend of mine." I couldn't bring myself to say Eric's name.

"I'm going to be very, very frank, sir," I say emphatically. "Are you the one who brought the assassin here AND ..." I raise my voice to stop him from his impatient, defensive interruption "and can you get him to leave this city?"

"GET OUT!" he shouts at me.

"I think I have what I came for, sir," I said quietly, even menacingly. I get up and begin walking toward the door. Then I turn and say, "Get rid of him or you will spend the rest of your life in prison."

It is a threat, I know, and I'm not sure how I can ever fulfill it. But it's worth catapulting him into a frenzy.

With that I leave.

Stanley Mosley picks up his phone. "Get rid of that meddlesome priest, NOW!" he shouts.

43

Surprise, surprise. My visitor this evening is none other than Margaret Mosley.

"Father Mike," she says with tears in her eyes, "first I want to apologize for the way I treated you the other day. I was totally out of line, petty and obnoxiously arrogant."

"Apology accepted," I say to her. "I know you were suffering from stress and I'm sure your stress right now is far worse because of the unhinged craziness of … well, of recent events."

I still could not bring myself to speak freely of Eric's murder.

Margaret crumbles into the chair I pointed to. "I love Eric," she cries, tears flooding her face. I really do … did … do love Eric. I wanted to marry him. But I knew he would never leave the priesthood.

"But I could still love him, even if only from a distance. And now … now, all I have is the memory."

I could tell from her unsheathed sincerity that the painful thrust of memory is cutting into her heart like a machete.

"Father Mike, I've come to tell you something very serious, something that could blow this town apart like a tornado."

"What is it, Margaret?" I ask gently. Mentally, I'm kicking myself for having rash judged this young, beautiful woman. And I am convinced that she truly loved Eric which breaks my heart – for both of them.

God bless celibacy.

"Father Mike, my father is behind the killing of Charles Sterling."

"How do you know that," I ask. She has just confirmed my suspicion, my intuition.

"Father, my father doesn't even know I exist. Even when he's looking at me, he doesn't see me. My mother dies during my birth. He has never forgiven me for that. My father is as cruel as Attila the Hun. He is as ruthless as Stalin. I know this is terrible to say but it's the truth."

"Try to relax," I say to her as kindly as I can.

"You ask me how I know my father is a murderer. Because he ignores me habitually, I have the run of the house. I go wherever I want. So I eavesdrop on his conversations, his phone calls, the comings and goings of his henchmen. I know almost everything that goes on in his activities.

"I tap into his phones, at home and, believe it or not, in his office. I heard him hiring that assassin. I have a tape …"

"You do?" I couldn't help myself.

"Yes. And I'm telling you this because he's ordered your death too.

49

So, I'm thinking, it's no longer Charon's personal vendetta. He's getting paid to kill me. I feel myself physically shaking. It's like a overwhelming feeling of emptiness, tugging at me, alternating between anger and fear.

Fear that I've been carrying around ever since Scuds told me Charon was after me. And anger at Margaret's father. That smooth magnate, pillar of society, devotee of the arts, benevolent philanthropist. That heartless murderer.

Margaret is sobbing again and I offer her tissues. I get up and put my hand on her shoulder. She reaches up and touches my hand so gently, dare I say, lovingly.

This poor little rich girl. All the material things she could ever want. But no love from a father who is so busy making the money that gives her all these things that he has no time for her.

"I accused him of having Eric killed," she cried. Probably at the mention of his name. That is not unreasonable. "As my father said, he doesn't care who I'm having a fling with. Told me to take a trip around the world. Oh God ... I just can't believe that man, that wonderful, charming man, is dead."

Again she burst into torrential tears.

I hate to interfere with her mourning, but I needed those tapes. I wait for a long while until she seems to get control of herself.

"My father even called someone and told him I knew about Charon and Sterling."

"Margaret," I say in my most solicitous voice, "do you have those phone tapes?"

"Yes, They're in a box in the bank. I put all of them in there."

"Could you ... would you get them for me? We ..." I emphasized the pronoun ... "need to bring the people who are responsible for Eric's death to justice, even if it means your father."

"I don't care about him. He's a criminal. Yes, I'll get them for you first thing tomorrow morning."

"Good. I don't know what to say to you. You're under such vulnerable stress. I know to tell you to pray sounds like a worn-out bromide ..."

"I have been praying. I'm praying to Eric ..." Another explosive outburst of tears.

"Keep praying to him, Margaret," I say as soothingly as I could.

"I'd better get back home. Not that anyone cares."

Margaret gets up. We embrace and I see her to the door.

No sooner had she stepped out into the night than there is a crack and she slumps to the ground.

My first reaction is to run to her. Once again my guards pull me from the door. Then I realize that the sniper is still there probably waiting for me. I dial my cell and call Detective Masconi.

She and Detective Morissey arrive within what seems to be minutes. They have backups.

They and their backups check the area and then check Margaret. Alison calls to me as I continue to stand just inside the doorway, "She's dead, Father. Shot through the head." Alison was as matter-of-fact as usual. No emotion whatsoever.

Detective Morissey says, as he holds out his hand, "The chewing gum wrapper again."

50

I stand frozen in place. I had just talked with her. Minutes ago. And now …

Who could be responsible for this? Her own father?. She told me that he knew about her having information about Charon and Sterling.

My God! Could he be, as Margaret said, as ruthless as Stalin?

The two detectives come into the rectory. We sit down. I pour myself an ample glass of bourbon. The detectives decline. "On duty," they say.

I sit there turning the glass between my fingers but not drinking.

Finally, I tell them all that Margaret told me, including and especially what she said about her father.

It's obvious that the two detectives are feeling some shock. More so than I did since I already believed what she told me about her father, but still I experience some shock in the details she told me.

"Father Mike," Alison says after she gets control, "all we have is the story Margaret Mosley told you. And that from a woman who felt neglected by the father she was accusing."

"In other words, no proof," I said with no little fatalism. I then tell them about my visit to Stanley Mosley and what my intuition tells me.

Again, Detective Morissey says, "Still no proof. We could never, ever arrest him based on what you claim Miss Mosley told you or your intuition."

Once more, I hear the sirens plowing through the dark night.

When is this going to stop? I wonder. With my death, no doubt.

As I tell the detectives, there is proof but I have no idea what bank Margaret has … had … a deposit box in. And no way of finding out as far as I can see.

The two detectives take their leave. I sit in suffocating silence. I am all alone. Skip Hecken is off for a few days. So here I sit.

For the first time in my life, I think, I feel lonely. It's a time when I question the sanity of celibacy.

But then if I had a wife, would I be telling her any of this? God bless celibacy?

51

I receive a call from Christine Joyce, Lulu's sister, who's been running Forrow House since Gloria died of cancer.

I haven't heard from her for quite a while. Ever since that murder of one of the residents at Forrow House.

She asks if I could come by.

I welcome the opportunity. I'm negligent as far as Forrow House is concerned. I can use a distraction.

But the distraction isn't the one I am looking for.

Christine announces that she will be leaving. She is going to marry McClan Dorrister, the orthopedic surgeon, she is dating.

"It's not that I don't like working here," she says rather mournfully, "but McClan wants to move out of the city. In fact, we've already purchased a home. It's beautiful.

Father Mike, I want you to marry us."

"Okay," I say slowly, letting her in on my disappointment. Then immediately I feel regret. It would be very selfish of me to have her stay here for the rest of her life.

I should be profoundly grateful for the time she has volunteered. It's just that she has been so good in this ministry. A replacement won't be easy.

As if reading my thoughts, Christine says, "I won't leave before we hire someone to take my place. In fact, I'll be glad to do the interviews. You have enough on your plate.

I don't know if she means my busy schedule at St. Ignatius or the threat from the assassin, Charon.

"Christine," I say sincerely, "I can't thank you enough for all you've done here. You are a true angel of mercy. The way you have turned some of these women around is as close to a miracle as I have ever seen."

"Thank you, Father Mike, you don't know how much that means to me. You will have our wedding?"

"Absolutely," I say, "wouldn't have it any other way. I consider it a privilege to be asked."

"You're such a gem," Christine says with a slight laugh.

"When will you begin the interviews?" I ask.

"Tomorrow," she replies. "I have set up the criteria. I'd appreciate it if you'd look them over."

"Will do. Well, I must be getting back."

With that we embraced. I'm certain I feel the spirit of Christine's sister present in our embrace. Lulu whom I still love as the daughter I never had. Lulu who was killed by my close friend Jim by mistake because she was trying to capture the killer by working under cover as a prostitute.

I whisper a prayer for Christine and McClan – and for Lulu.

52

I keep mulling over what Detective Masconi said about not having proof of Stanley Mosley's at least collaboration.

I'm also wondering how he is taking the death, the murder, of his only daughter, his only child.

Did he order her murder or just go along with it for the betterment of his conglomerate which is under federal investigation.

Since there is no legal way to prove Mosley's daughter's allegations, there is another way. That's why we make friends with Mammon.

I call Don Giovanni and ask for an appointment.

He gives it to me at once.

I head over to Tullio's where the Don holds court.

"Don Giovanni," I say with respect, "thank you for seeing me on such short notice."

"Anything for you, Father Mike," the Don says with the graciousness of carefree philanthropist.

I sit down and tell him the whole tale, emphasizing what Margaret Mosley told me and how the police said there is no proof.

"And what you want is proof?" Don Giovanni asks with intense attention as if he were plotting to take over city government.

"Can you help me?" I ask again with sincere respect.

"Consider it done," says the Don.

Unknown to me, but I later find out, Don Giovanni had to report to the Cardinal that he had made no headway in finding Charon.

This is a deep, red-faced embarrassment for the Don.

"I will not tell you what I am going to do," the Don says, pulling down the invisible cone of silence over himself.

"I just want proof that Mosley is behind these murders, that he hired Charon."

"You will have your proof. I guarantee it," the Don smiles.

I thank him, not too profusely and I leave Tullio's and head for home, wondering if there is a bullet waiting for me somewhere along the way.

My guards are with me but ...

53

According to Petey the Weasel, one of Don Giovanni's right hand henchmen, this is how it went down.

I'm certain that the Don instructed Petey to tell me so that I would appreciate the Don's efficiency.

Stanley Mosley is entering his car to go to his office.

Two of the Don's men knock out Mosley's driver as three others grab Mosley and inject something into Mosley's neck which immediately knocks him unconscious.

When Mosley wakes up, he's in some kind of a dungeon, his arms tied behind a chair, his feet bound, his mouth taped shut and a heavy blindfold covers his eyes.

Petey the Weasel is in charge of the interrogation.

The Don distances himself from such events inasmuch as he detests violence.

Mosley moans. He urinates in his pants. Turns red with embarrassment or with fury.

Petey pulls the tapes away from Mosley's mouth and eyes.

A big mistake if you don't want to hear compulsive screaming.

"Who are you thugs?" Mosley screams.

"Shut up," Petey snaps but to no avail.

"What do you crazies want?" again he shouts like dry barking.

"We crazies want you to confess," Petey shouts back at him.

"Confess? Confess to what? For God's sake!" Mosley is now sweating profusely.

"We want you to confess to the murders of Charles Sterling, Monsignor Stouffer and your own daughter."

"You're out of your mind!" Still shouting.

"We want you to confess to bringing Charon to our city and paying him to assassinate these people and to put a price on the head of Father Michael," Petey is as firm in his demands as a newly promoted Major in the military. He is totally no nonsense.

"You had better release me NOW! I have resources. I'll have you tracked down."

"Shut up with your threats," Petey shouts back. "Just give us the information we want and you can go."

"Go to hell!" Mosley isn't budging.

"Mr. Mosley," Petey purrs, "you're not getting out of here alive until you confess."

"What good would my confession be? It would have been forced through duress. It wouldn't stand up in any court."

"Not your courts, but there are others," Petey's now smug.

"I don't know what you mean."

"Well, think about it. We'll be back in a while."

"Could I have some water," Mosley is begging.

"You must be kiddin'." Petey smiles in such a way that it should send throbbing tremors through the staunchest of men.

54

Petey returns.

"Give some thought to your confession?" Petey asks, showing no signs of impatience.

"Go to hell." This time Mosley whimpers.

"Okay," Petey says. "Josh, untie Mr. Mosley's arms."

"Thank you," Mosley says, still whimpering.

"Josh," Petey says, "bring over that table and put it in front of Mr. Mosley. Now put Mr. Mosley's right hand on the table and hold it there."

"What are you going to do?" Mosley sounds as if his voice is frozen in mounds of fear.

And well should it be.

"Brad," Petey orders, "cut off Mr. Mosley's thumb."

"Noooo," Mosley screams.

"Are you having second thoughts, Mr. Mosley?"

"I … I can't stand pain. Let me pay you. I can give you millions of dollars. Millions!" Never in his life has he begged like he is at this moment.

"Cut off his thumb," Petey orders with the finality of an avenging angel.

Mosley twists in the chair. Tries to pull his hand away. All the while screaming and crying.

Finally, breathless and exhausted, Mosley caves in.

"All right, all right." Almost a heaving sigh. "I'll tell you what you want to know. Please don't torture me.

55

"A very wise decision, Mr. Mosley." Petey is sneering.

"Josh bring over the recorder and put it on the table."

"Now, Mr. Mosley, state your name, your position and the date of the year.

Mosley does as he is commanded.

"Now, Mr. Mosley, tell the audience what you done and I want details, not a sketch." Petey says almost soothingly.

"I hired an assassin named Charon to kill Charles Sterling."

"Details," Petey's voice is deep, commanding, authoritative, intimidating and yet in a strange way paternal.

"Our company is under investigation by the Securities and Exchange Commission. Sterling made an appointment with the Commission. He was going to blow the whistle on us.

"He was on his way. I told Charon when and where. He took care of the rest."

"And Monsignor Stouffer?" Petey asks.

"I know nothing about that. If Charon killed him, that's his decision. I only met Stouffer once, at a fund raiser. I've been told that my daughter is … was … having an affair with Stouffer. I don't know any more. I swear to God."

"And your daughter?" Petey sounded more like a policeman than a member of the Don's "group."

"That is a regretful matter. She knows … knew … just too much. She was angry with me. Accused me of ordering Stouffer's killing. I didn't. It was too precarious. She knew enough to blow the whistle on us."

"So you ordered Charon to take out your own daughter?" Petey almost sounds shocked.

"Yes," and Mosley breaks down and cries uncontrollably, a lonely soul locked in the prison of his own greed.

When Mosley finishes crying, Petey asks, "And what about Father Mike?"

"I don't know what you're referring to," Mosley says in a determined voice.

"Charon's out to kill Father Mike," Petey says as simply as if telling Mosley his address.

"All I know about this Father Mike is that he's a snooping busybody. He's always playing the clever sleuth. He should stick to running his parish instead of running around interrogating people in good standing."

"In good standing like you?" Petey sneers.

"Your daughter told Father Mike you ordered Charon to take him out," Petey says dogmatically.

"Okay, okay, I did." Mosley gives up trying to lie. He just wants out.

With that Petey signals Josh who injects Mosley once again in the neck. They make copies of Mosley's confession. Then stick a copy of his confession into his coat pocket.

They put him in a van, drive to the police station and dump him outside in the back.

As they drive away, Petey calls the station. "Outside behind your building, you'll find a man with a tape of his confession in his inside pocket. Go get him." Abruptly Petey clicks off.

56

I drop in to Forrow Haven.

"How're the interviews coming?" I ask Christine.

"I am busy," she says with a wan smile.

"Have you come to any decision?" I ask.

"I have one woman in mind. I don't know if you'll approve."

"You're the one to do the hiring. I have total confidence in your judgment."

"Well," Christine says, as she takes a deep breath, "the woman is a former prostitute. Then she became a madam. Then she totally turned her life around. Right now she is working as an executive secretary at Bradford and Bradford Octogenic Chemicals. She is the personal private chief assistant to the CEO, Stanley Mosley.

"I'm thinking that with her background as a madam she would make the ideal house mother here at Forrow Haven. What do you think, Father Mike?"

"You're sure she wouldn't turn Forrow Haven into ..."

"A whore house?" Christine laughed.

"Well ..."

"I'm certain that from her own experience she would want to help these women to follow her path of repentance and regeneration."

"Besides," Christine is doing a full court selling job, "she is a very compassionate and non judgmental person. They're very important qualities."

"Okay," I say without a load of conviction. But I try to present at least a veneer of compliance.

Christine seems relieved. Very relieved.

Then she says, "I'm really going to miss this place. I'll miss the interaction with the residents. The help I think I'm giving them."

"May I ask her name?"

"Mavis Sullivan," Christine smiles. "Would you like to meet her?"

"She's here? Now?"

"She is. When you said you were coming over, I called her and asked her to come in."

"Well ... yes, I would like to meet her," I say hesitantly. I offer a quick prayer asking God to help me to be non judgmental.

57

"Hello, Father Mike, it's so good to meet you. I've hear wonderful things about you. Forrow Haven? How you were able to bring this about, I'll never know. It's just too wonderful. I wish I had such a blessing."

Such effusion. She all but canonizes me.

Mavis Sullivan is a very attractive woman. Probably in her mid fifties but well preserved. Brown hair and eyes. High cheek bones and a very easy wide smile. She is shapely yet not heavy.

I have a very quirky yet unkind thought: I'll bet she made a bundle in her former profession.

"Miss Sullivan, I'm glad to meet you too," I say easily, sincerely.

"Mavis, please," she says back to me with exuding charm.

"May I ask you how long you have been …"

"Out of the profession?" She laughs slightly, perhaps at my obvious embarrassment.

"Over eleven years. Actually several years more since I became a madam."

She certainly was open and not the least hesitant about her past.

"Do you have any religious beliefs?" I ask unobtrusively.

"Sullivan, Father Mike. Irish Catholic. Not practicing for most of my life, but back into it, at least formally if not intensely."

Quite articulate.

"Christine speaks highly of you, Mavis. That's good enough for me."

"I hope, if I'm hired, you will still continue to be involved in Forrow Haven, Father Mike."

"I intend to be, Mavis. And may God bless you in your new work."

"Then I'm hired?" Mavis looks at Christine who nods her head positively.

Mavis rushes over and embraces me. Then she steps back quickly, apologizing. I say it's all right. Embracing has a therapeutic value.

"I can begin in four weeks," Mavis says. "I wish it could be sooner. I can't stand my present job, working for that crook, Stanley Mosley, but I have to give four weeks notice."

"Good," Christine and I say together. although I don't miss Mavis' negative reference to Mosley.

I must admit that I leave feeling quite comfortable about Christine's choice. Although I am feeling a bit down about Christine's leaving Forrow Haven. I hope the residents will take it well. Christine hasn't told them yet. They should be receptive to Mavis. I hope so. I pray so.

58

The police drag Mosley inside.

They get a doctor who injects Mosley with something that brings him out of his stupor.

Detectives Morissey and Masconi are called in.

They listen to Mosley's confession on the tape.

They look at one another, not knowing whether to cheer or doubt.

Mosley immediately asks for his lawyer.

Sebastian MacAfee races to the precinct. "Are you arresting my client?" he asks in a haughty, demeaning tone.

"Not at this time," Morissey answers.

"Come, Mr. Mosley," MacAfee says in the most solicitous tone.

"Don't even think of leaving the city," Masconi warns.

Mosley stares at the two detectives and sneers. "You'll be hearing from me. You can take that to the bank."

"We have to take this tape to the DA," Alison Masconi states as nonchalantly as a football player gaining a few yards by simply falling forward.

"This guy regards murder with the indifference of a meter maid dispensing parking tickets." Morissey says.

"I'll bet the DA tells us that the confession was gained under duress and is unadmisable," Masconi observes.

As they expect, the DA says the recording would not hold up in court.

"Our problem," Alison Masconi says, "is the flight risk. Mosley could hop a private jet and head to any country where there is no extradition."

"Okay," the DA says, "pick him up. We might get the judge to deny bail. But it's a long shot.

59

Today is fill in day.

First, Petey the Weasel comes to see me. He tells me everything that happened. He also tells me the Don sends his best regards and hopes I can get some peace.

I thank Petey. He leaves and goes back to wherever.

Next, I call Alison Masconi. She fills me in on letting Mosley go and how they are going to arrest him to at least try to keep him from fleeing.

Later in the day, Alison calls me back.

"We arrested him," she says. "Conspiracy to murder. He's due in court tomorrow morning. I don't know what to expect. I hate to think it's hopeless." She sighs deeply. She's either very tired or quite hopeless. It's hard to tell."

"There's a good chance the judge will throw out the tape," Alison moans. "Confession under duress etc. But that's up to the judge." Again a sigh of what sounded like hopelessness or maybe just plain helplessness.

Being a detective has its downsides.

The next day, I go to the court house.

Mosley's lawyer puts up a good argument, but the judge buys the DA's pitch on flight risk. The DA points out that taking Mosley's passport doesn't do any good since Mosley has access to private jets. Plural: jets!

So the judge remands him. Score one for our side.

Then the judge orders one of those electronic ankle bracelets put on Mosley.

I'm bewildered. If Mosley's going into a cell, why the bracelet. Maybe the judge is worried that Mosley will find a way out of jail and try to flee.

But if he can find a way out jail, he certainly will find someone who can remove the bracelet.

Then there's the tape. If that tape won't cut it in court, Mosley will probably go free.

It's all so tenuous.

I'm sitting in my study, turning all the information over and over and coming up with a proverbial goose egg.

Then the obvious dawns on me. Mavis Sullivan. How can I ever thank God enough for my intuition?

Could she ...? Would she ...?

I'm planning to go to Forrow Haven first thing after Mass tomorrow morning.

60

"I don't know, Father Mike," Mavis says as hesitantly as a child fearing to tackle a math problem.

"I'm in the process of preparing for my new job or ministry, as Christine calls it. I don't want to get into trouble."

"What kind of trouble could you get into?" I ask feeling as helpless as being caught in a bottomless sea.

"Look what they did to Mr. Sterling, Father Mike. They had him killed."

"You know that for certain?" I ask.

"Of course, I know just about everything that goes on in that man, Mr. Mosley's, office."

"But," I insist as persuasively as what I'm being, a con man, "Mosley's in a jail cell. You can go into his office on any pretext, even getting some papers for him.

"What we desperately need is some proof of his criminal dealings. Without it he goes free, flies off to another country and God knows commits some more barbaric atrocities.

"We also need proof that he hired Charon. You're the only one who can get this proof. Once we have the proof, Mosley can be convicted and spend the rest of his life in prison. No harm will come to you."

Now I feel I'm lying to her. Mosley could as readily deliver orders from prison as a conductor leading a symphonic orchestra. He could still keep Charon on the payroll.

Still if we could put Mosley in prison, some of the horrendous activities might be mitigated.

"Well," Mavis says quietly, almost fatalistically, "I could try. You have to give me some kind of a list of what it is you want."

Good girl, I thought, but I say, "Thank you, Mavis. This is a very heroic act you are performing."

I want to add, I guarantee your safety, but I couldn't.

Right now I want to contact one of the detectives and tell them what is going on. I also want to see what protection they could give to Mavis, if any.

Mavis could get enough evidence to bring down the whole conglomerate.

And if Bradford and Bradford Octogenics could be destroyed, maybe Charon would go look for employment elsewhere.

Charon would certainly not work without getting paid – except in my case.

"You *what?*" Detective Alison Masconi shrieked.

It's the first time I have ever seen any emotion in Alison.

"It's the only thing I can think of," I say rather sheepishly, standing in front of her more like a whipped dog.

"This woman could get into a lot of trouble. She could be killed." Alison is still shrieking.

"You know what they did to Sterling," she says, repeating exactly what Mavis said. "Shot him down in broad daylight. Everyone knows he was on his way to the Securities and Exchange Commission to blow the whistle on Bradford and Bradford Octogenics. We just can't prove it."

"Precisely," I say, regaining some of my confidence. "What we need is proof. Now how do we get it? Torture Mosley again to get another confession that won't stand up in court."

Finally, Detective Masconi simmers down. She's thinking it through. She knows I'm right.

"Does she – this Mavis – know when she can get this information?" Alison asks.

I have her hooked.

"No, she is still a bit shaky. All we can do is pray that she has the courage to go through with it," I say, hoping I don't sound too pietistic. I mean it. Pray.

"How do we proceed?" Alison asks.

"Mavis will bring me whatever she gets and I bring it immediately to you, and then we – you – can call in the Feds," I say.

"I only hope she knows what to bring to you."

"I gave her a list," I reply.

"You did? How do you know what she is to get?" Alison asks with a little annoyance.

"More or less I depend on my intuition," I say to her.

"Your intuition, as I've been told, is almost foolproof. I hope it comes through in this case. We can't afford to botch this." Alison now seems as apprehensive as standing on the edge of a high dive.

"I always trust my intuition. My intuition comes from long times of contemplating the various cases I've been involved in within my prayer. I also find that my intuitions break in on me during times of leisure when I'm consciously thinking about something else, something unrelated."

"Well, I guess you're blessed with some kind of sixth sense, unless you believe God speaks directly to you."

"*Alison*," I say in a pleading tone.

Alison smiles at me which seems to be a stretch between belief and skepticism.

"Let's hope Mavis is able to get whatever information we need," I sigh.

"Can she get into his computer?" Alison asks, still not entirely convinced.

"She says she can," I tell her, trying to bolster her confidence in Mavis and in me.

"As soon as you get whatever, get it to me so we can go through it. I hope we can get this bastard. If we can get him for conspiracy in murder, we'll put him away for a very long time."

She does seem hopeful if not confident.

61

I remember reading that if we keep doing what we have always done, we will be what we have always been.

I recognize how much I need courage to go through with this plan. Actually, Mavis is the one who needs the courage.

I pray that she would have the courage to get the proof we so desperately need.

As far as the threat that continues to hang over me, I also realize that it takes less courage to face death than life.

That's easier said than lived.

I also realize that to face whatever the future holds for me, even my death, I must confront the present with courage.

So I have to confront the present situation of Charon plotting to kill me.

The word, kill, sends bone-crushing chills throughout my whole being.

The problem with this present is that even if Mosley is convicted, even if Bradford and Bradford Octogenics goes into bankruptcy, that is no guarantee of my personal safety.

I must find Charon.

How? I have no idea.

As I am mulling over my quandary, the phone rings.

"Hello, Father Mike," Don Giovanni almost sings my name.

"Hello, Don," I say with respect.

"I have some information for you."

"I'll be right over," I say again with respect.

I find the Don in his usual place at Tullio's.

"Yes?" I say to the Don.

"Please, Father Mike, have a seat."

"Don, I want to thank you for your efforts with Stanley Mosley," I say.

"It was nothin'," the Don says. "But I am given to understand that the confession's no good."

"The DA says it was forced and wouldn't stand up in court," I sigh.

Then I tell the Don about Mavis and what I hope she will be able to find.

"But that doesn't get you from under Charon, Father Mike," the Don knows he's telling me the obvious.

"I'm thinking about that very thing," I say obviously disheartened.

"Well," the Don smiles mysteriously, "I have information that wasn't in the tape.

Petey kept it for me."

"And that is?" I ask hopefully.

"Petey got the contact number out of that scum, Mosley."

"The contact number?" I'm amazed.

"The same," the Don smiles reassuringly.

62

After a brief discussion about what to do with this contact number, it was decided that I should bring it to the detectives.

At first, the Don wanted to send the message.

He is most persuasive.

But I insist that I want to let the police know.

The Don doesn't have any trust in the police, but finally he concedes, reserving for himself the right to make contact since he is the one who first got the number.

We depart on good terms as always.

I am almost breathless in telling the two detectives about the contact number. I say to them, "We're at a crossroads. Hunting down and capturing Charon or going after Mosley for complicity in murder."

Both Morissey and Masconi agree that the first thing to be done is to go after Charon.

They also agree that I am the one to make the contact.

And so I do. I can't help but notice that my hands are trembling.

I punch in the number

Finally, I get through. I get a message. "You have reached Pickwick Antiques. Leave your number and someone will get back to you."

I am stupefied. I didn't think about this.

I'm frozen. I don't know what number to leave. Any number could be traced.

In a momentary inspiration or desperation, I leave the Don's private computer address.

I turn to the two detectives who are wondering what is going on and explain what had just happened.

Then I say, "I better call Don Giovanni and let him know what I have done."

Both detectives agree.

So I call the Don. I explain about the voice message and then I say to him, "Don, please don't be angry with me but the only number I could come up with is yours."

"Not angry, Father Mike. I am looking forward to having a conversation with that murdering scum."

I breathe a heavy sigh of relief and tell the detectives the Don's reaction.

"Good," they say in unison.

I literally wander back to the rectory, wondering how the Don is going to handle this – this mess.

Once again my thoughts are turning to the matter of death. More precisely my death.

I've been meditating quite a bit on Peter O'Toole's epitaph taken from a sign at the local cleaners: It distresses us to return work that is not perfect.

But God doesn't call us to be perfect. God calls us to holiness.

Striving for perfection sinks into perfectionism like leaky tanker on the ocean.

And perfectionism is itself a fault. It says, Here I am. By my own efforts I am faultless. Now, God, you must reward me.

Ironically, perfectionism is a form of the ancient heresy, Pelagianism which taught that we gain salvation by pulling ourselves up by our own bootstraps. No need for God's help. We can do it by ourselves. Do heresies ever die?

Perfectionism is absolutely unreasonable denial of our humanness. The marvelous gift God has bestowed on us, our humanness.

Oh, well, I have to resign myself to what will be. If Charon does succeed in killing me, one thing for sure, I'll never be canonized as a martyr like Archbishop Romero hasn't been to the universal embarrassment of our Church.

63

It was early evening when the door chimes ring.

I go to the door.

The Cardinal ordered me to get a new door, doors actually, with peep holes in the new doors, so I could see who was outside. And so I did. The Cardinal likes obedience.

I look through and standing there is Detective Masconi.

I open the door. "Detective Masconi," I say with genuine delight, "how nice to see you."

"Well," she says, "I don't know how nice it is."

I freeze. What now?

"Please, come in," I say to her.

"I'm here not on a professional level. It's personal."

I feel my body relax with relief like a punctured balloon.

"Come, let's go into the kitchen. We can have a cup of coffee or tea."

Alison was obviously tense. So I do some small talk. I really don't know anything about her personally, except she's as tough as Hercules. Nothing seems to be able to shake her.

Yet, here she is seeming almost as vulnerable as my small Himalayan kitten, Bridget.

She's a beautiful little cat. Someone gave her to me because they were moving into an apartment and pets were not allowed.

She is so funny that no matter what crosses I endure during the day, I can sit, relax and laugh at her antics.

God bless celibacy.

Finally, I say to her, "Alison, what's the matter?"

She inhales a sob.

"Some time ago, I was at a workshop. I met this detective from New York. All during the workshop, he's coming onto me. I must admit I was flattered.

"Father Mike, I was married and am divorced. It was a horrible mistake. From the beginning he ran around on me. Finally, I threw him out of the apartment. Then the divorce.

"Ever since, I haven't bothered with men. No flirting, no dating. Just keeping busy with my job.

"Now he wants to come here and 'take me out to dinner.' I don't know what to do."

She pauses. I'm supposing she wants me to say something.

"What do you know about him?" I ask

"Only what he told me," she sighs.

"Can you get more information on him?" I ask.

"Yes, I'm sure I can." She's looking wary.

"Did he say anything about being married, having a family."

"No, he gave me the impression that he's foot loose and fancy free, as the saying goes."

"My advice, Alison, is to track him down. Find out much more about him before giving him the green light for coming here. You know, there's more to this than dinner."

"Yes, I know. I just don't want to get hurt again. Once is for a lifetime. I guess I knew what I had to do. I just wanted to hear it from someone else. Thanks, Father Mike."

With small tears in her eyes, she gets up to leave.

I walk her to the door. I look out through the peep hole. Although it's dark out, there are the blazing lights the Cardinal ordered me to have installed, which I did. The Cardinal likes obedience.

I'm at the point that I fear anyone leaving through the front door. A sick, hot squirming, claustrophobic fear.

Alison makes it to her car and drives off into the night. Puzzled but alive.

My heart aches for her. It's amazing how little we know about the people we interact with.

Often I stand at the pulpit and the altar, realizing that I don't know what people are going through: what crosses, what heartbreaks, what insoluble problems. I hope my homilies touch them in some way.

My impression of Alison is that of a rock as solid as Gibraltar. But she is just another vulnerable human being, searching for happiness, craving love, warding off loneliness day in day out, and every long night.

Alison is a pretty young woman. She deserves love. I pray that she will find it one day.

Maybe this New York detective is legit. Maybe not.

That's up to Alison to find out.

I find over the long haul that when I give advice, I have to be ready to hear that person say something like, "I really don't need your advice right now. Please just be sensitive to my feelings at the moment."

I remember seeing an episode of "Star Trek, The Next Generation."

Picard says to Data, "I would like to give you all the advice I can. When I have some, I'll let you know."

Sometimes we are too quick, even glib, in handing out advice.

I often wonder if it's a need for us to feel important, even indispensable. A striving for some kind of immortality.

I know priests who in the confessional try to solve everyone's problems, even if they haven't told the priest their problem.

It seems to me that such advising should be done in the parish office. How many people would bother to make an appointment?

Sometimes their problems are as fleeting as clouds in a summer sky.

Another thought I'm pondering is that we should not take people's problems as our own.

It's my mother's famous advice again: about not going to my room worried about someone I tried to help in the office while that person goes home whistling.

Next to giving unsolicited advice is shoving our advice down somebody's throat, expecting someone to follow our advice lockstep without question.

One time while I am ministering to an old man who was dying, he said to me, "Are you expecting some deathbed advice? Well here it is: don't get old before your time.

"Sometimes we live our lives too fast, like skimming through a novel. You remember the plot but can't remember the whole story. That's a sad way to live."

I wonder if he was talking about himself.

There and then I resolve to stop and look at flowers, stare up at the stars, relax in the love of friends.

Right now I am wondering if I will never have the chance to grow old too fast.

64

"You called," the voice sounds hesitant, almost wavering.

"Yes, is this youse?" Don Giovanni answers.

"Yes," came the reply. "How did you get this number?"

"I am Don Giovanni. How I get dis number is not yur concern. The only ting youse have to be concerned about is the job I want youse to do.

Don Giovanni likes to sound next to illiterate. He believes it keeps the other person off guard. They underestimate the Don which puts him in control.

At least this is what he believes.

Charon never takes direct calls. He made one exception: Mosley. So, he guessed, he could make this exception too.

"What's the job?" the voice gruffly asks.

"Der's sombuddy I need to meet his maker. I don't want it traced back here. So I'm willin' to hire."

"If I take the job, it'll cost you."

"Shur. I know dat. You tink I'm a moran?"

154

"No offense," the voice a bit more mellow. "Since you're the Don, I'm giving you a deal. Two hundred thou. Half now, half after the job. To be deposited in my Swiss bank account."

"Now," the voice, Charon's voice continues, "I need three different pictures of the target and details of his or her life, comings and goings, places. I also need a written report as to why you want him taken out. You get the order."

"How will I get dis info to youse?"

"You don't get them to me. You mail the information to a mailbox, The number is 242213 in the main branch of the Post Office. The name is Joseph Quigley."

"Youse don't have much trust," the Don griped.

"Trust is your character flaw, not mine," Charon utters a stifled laugh.

"How soon?" The Don sounds impatient.

"Within five days," comes the answer.

"This ain't much time," the Don complains..

"I'm a busy man. Five days or forget it." Charon is definitive.

"All right," the Don pretends to whine.

They disconnect with not so much as a goodbye.

Don Giovanni looks up at Petey the Weasel.

"We couldn't get a trace, Don. He must of used a cloned phone," Petey says expecting an explosion.

"That's okay," the Don smiles. "I have a better plan."

65

There is always a bright spot in any darkness.

Charon's pursuit of me, his insane violence, his insatiable wickedness makes me more aware of my need to continue my work of peacemaking.

Sometimes we don't realize that Christian values are not the only ones that can insure our progress in spirituality.

I remember reading Naim Ateek's insight from his work, *Justice, and Only Justice: A Palestinian Theology of Liberation*, The word for peace in both Arabic (salam) and Hebrew (shalom) has the same etymological root and the same breadth of meaning: wholeness, health, safety, and security. It refers to a peace experienced and lived out in the everyday historical situation of life. Peace can be a basis or cause that leads to something else. It is either a prerequisite or a by-product.

I don't think we should be surprised at someone like Charon.

Charon is a symbol of the barbaric violence throughout the world, the savage killings and murders that are sanctioned by national governments.

If I work for or preach on peace, there are people who accuse me of introducing politics into my homilies.

Of course, they are coming from a viewpoint that says we should just preach about otherworldly things. We should not make connections between the gospel story and what is going on in our world or lives here and now.

How can a priest preach on peace without citing the horrific consequences of warfare wherever it is being waged as in Columbia today?

People don't seem to mind if we talk about peace in theory. But we should not bring up actual examples of the opposite of peace: war with all the men and women who are being ruthlessly killed or wounded beyond recovery for a normal life.

And how our governmental leaders use euphemisms to cover up reality! They talk about our brave soldiers who are sacrificing their lives.

The reality is that these soldiers are having their lives brutally taken away from them not sacrificing them.

If, as Jesus says, peacemakers are happy, there must be millions of people throughout the world who are desperately unhappy.

I know from experience that in my efforts to bring about a keener awareness of the need to be peacemakers, I am called a malcontent, a rabble-rouser, a traitor.

It's easy to accept the gospel as long as it doesn't disrupt our lives, our comfort, our compromises with our culture's values.

I recall something Archbishop Romero said. "A church that doesn't provoke crises, a Gospel that doesn't unsettle, a word of God that doesn't get under anyone's skin are just very nice, pious considerations that don't bother anyone. That's the way many would like preaching to be. Those preachers who avoid every thorny matter so as not to be harassed do not light up the world they live in."

Just preach about getting to heaven, Father. Don't be talking about peace and war, starving and hated people.

God help us all!

66

It seems to me that the imperative of peacemaking is tied closely to working for justice. And this is what I preach and what I'm going to preach despite its being a 'thorny matter.'

Whatever is unjust threatens peace.

There can be no peace where there is injustice toward those in our society who are not cared for, the throwaways, the runaways, the destitute, the disenfranchised, the marginalized, the forgotten.

All those thrown on the garbage heap of life.

There will always be an uprising from the poor and neglected against those who have more.

I'm convinced we need to ask not what the poor require, but what do we who are better off really need.

I read somewhere that $540,000 tax dollars were given for research on onions while five million children go to bed every night hungry here in the United States, the richest nation on the earth..

The apathy toward peacemaking is disguised as loyalty to our government. For many, when the flag is raised, they immediately salute, even mindlessly salute.

It always blows my mind how people who claim to believe in Jesus and accept his teachings, make decisions without ever consulting the gospel values.

In effect, they are saying: That's the gospel. We're talking about real life.

It's amazing to me how easily our culture seduces so-called people of faith into its values.

Perhaps they're easily seduced because in fact they're people of religion.

The peace Jesus preached should cause people of faith to have an itching discontent because the world is not what it should be.

G.K. Chesterton, in one of his more obvious paradoxes, said: "We must hate the world and love the world at the same time. We hate the world enough to want to change it for the better. We love the world enough to believe it's worth making better."

I think that human life is considered so cheap, so taken for granted and treated with such active disregard that it can be thrown on the sewer of death without a bit of remorse, without a thought.

From my readings, peacemaking is not some ideal in far off never-never land. It's a here and now challenge.

To search for peace means we have to ask tough questions about the value we place or do not give to human life.

Where there is injustice, terrorism, warfare, there must be peacemakers who will stand up and speak truth to power, saying, "Enough!"

It's so simple for old men to sit around sending young men off to spill their blood for political and economic power plays and call it patriotism.

In war, young people die and older people talk. In war, older men send young men off to battle, while they sit around, drinking their cocktails and checking the poll numbers.

Charon is not the only madman on the loose.

The other evening I am rooting through some papers I still have to file.

I come across a quote from Martin Luther King from his famous speech against the Vietnam War given in 1967:

"Even when pressed by the demands of inner truth, men do not easily assume the task of opposing their government's policy, especially in time of war. Nor does the human spirit move without great difficulty against all the apathy of conformist thought ..."

To be a peacemaker in the spirit of the non violent Christ means risk. It is the true launching out into the deep.

There are so many so-called patriots who allow themselves to be brainwashed by whatever those in power in our country tell us, for example, that to go against these power-mongers is considered an act of collusion with whatever enemy those in power are demonizing.

Then there is the brainwashing of our young men and women, turning them into killers. The enemy is demonized and our young military people are told over and over that they must kill the enemy.

Charon is not the only madman on the loose.

By a curious twist of paradox, Charon is more honest in his killings than our political leaders are in theirs.

Sadly, I have to admit that my own church is not always out in the forefront protesting war and championing peace.

The leadership of the Church is always cautious, waiting to see how the wind is blowing. The Church leaders seem to play catch up with the people they're leading.

This makes it all the more difficult for an ordinary parish priest to speak out.

Although I must admit the leaders, at least ours, don't interfere with the parish priest's speaking out against war or against the government for that matter.

I guess it's a kind of backdoor support. Who knows how it works way up there on Mt. Olympus?

67

"Yur Eminence," Don Giovanni speaks with proper respect as one who values respect very highly, "I had some problem getting through to you."

"Don, I told Monsignor Bevins to put you through immediately."

"Well, Eminence, he grilled me. I don't go for dat."

"Be assured, Don, Monsignor Bevins will hear from me. I don't go for that either."

Suddenly the Don switched from his farce of the idiom and diction of the not too educated into clearly spoken English.

"Your Eminence, I can tell you I have a plan to get this assassin, Charon. Obviously I can't go into the plan. Let it be enough that you know there is a plan in action."

"I can't express my gratitude sufficiently," the Cardinal purred. "I owe you big time."

"Just pray for me. That will be enough."

Then Don Giovanni alters his tone to one of a worn-down soul. No longer does he sound like the dictator but like a down-and-outer.

"Your Eminence, do you think there is hope for me? You know ... with my work and all."

"Don," the Cardinal speaks soothingly, "God is infinitely merciful. God is boundlessly forgiving."

"I know," the Don says plaintively, "but my life isn't exactly a saint's."

"Don, do you remember the good thief on the cross next to Jesus?"

"Yeah, sure, but he was really sorry."

"Can you be sorry?" the Cardinal asks, exerting his best pastoral concern.

"I don't know. I don't think so." There's a touch of anguish in his tone.

"Well, then," the Cardinal persists, "can you be sorry for not being sorry?"

"Yeah, I guess I can do that," the Don sounds hopeful. "Sorry for not being sorry. Yeah I can really do that. Do you think God would take that?"

"Don, all you have to do is accept the mercy and forgiveness God is already extending to you by repenting of the sins that have separated or are separating you from God."

"Repenting," the Don repeats. "That's where I think I might have problems. I don't feel repenting. I'm not even sure what repenting is."

"It's being sorry, Don."

"Even if it's being sorry for not being sorry?" Again the Don sounds plaintive.

"Even so, Don." The Cardinal is being gently pastoral, no doubt trying to repay the debt he thinks he owes Don Giovanni.

"Don," the Cardinal continues, "we can be honest about our sinfulness when we recognize God's infinite mercy. Our God does not give us what we deserve. Instead of punishment, our God is constantly extending us endless mercy."

"I wish I could believe that," the Don says.

"My dear Don," the Cardinal insists, "God's mercy builds a bridge between our doubts about his boundless forgiveness and trust in his loving embrace of absolution.

"Think of Jesus' parable about the Prodigal son. Remember how the father didn't wait for his son to make it home, but ran down the hill to embrace his son with forgiving love.

"The father didn't even let his son finish his act of contrition, but instantly forgave him.

"Jesus was revealing God the Father and his infinite mercy."

"That's beautiful, Eminence. No wonder they made you a Cardinal."

63

"Getting back to your initial message, Don, if I may," the Cardinal is respectful. "I know you can't tell me what your plan is, but how sure are you that your plan will work?"

"It'll work, Eminence, or some of my boys will be meeting their all-merciful God a lot sooner than they expect."

The Cardinal couldn't help but laugh softly. Probably at the paradox within his conversation with the Don.

The Don, hearing the Cardinal's laughter, broke into a boisterous laugh himself. No doubt he too sees the contradiction.

"Good talking with you, Eminence."

"Call any time, Don, and I assure you direct access."

No sooner does the Cardinal disconnect than he summons Monsignor Bevins.

"Didn't I tell you that Don Giovanni has immediate access to me no matter what I am involved with?" His voice transparently revealed his anger.

Bevins just stands there, head bowed.

"It's Mike, isn't it? You're upset because I'm showing him preferential treatment. My God, man. His life is being threatened," his voice thundered.

"You don't approve of my dealing with the 'sordid' side of life, with the Don. Well, I tell you I would deal with Satan himself if it would assure Mike's safety.

"So, Monsignor, the pastor of St. Rocco's is retiring. Make preparations to take over the parish. Your service here is done."

With that the Cardinal waves his hand in an angry sign of dismissal.

69

The Don tells me about his conversation with the Cardinal.

He sounds beside himself. Thrilled with the Cardinal.

He also tells me he has a plan to get Charon, but can't go into details.

He also mentions that maybe someday he might come to confession to me. Would I be willing to hear his confession?

I answer yes most graciously.

He hangs up, a very satisfied man.

I'm happy for him.

Another one of those visits without an appointment.

People must think a priest has nothing to do all day except sit around waiting for someone to pop in like the sun bursting into radiant gold in the last moments of sunset.

Most of the time the people who pop are more like a gloom cloud eager to plunge the sun of the priest's day into endless cycles of dismal darkness.

This is one of those days.

My visitors are the Chairman and Vice Chairwoman of my parish council.

"Good morning, Alex and Sarah," I say trying to be as congenial as a candidate running for office.

Alex is a self-important, plump little man with an obvious Napoleonic complex.

Sarah is a shrinking violet who bows wherever Alex's wind blows.

"Is there something I can do for you?" This time I pick up some papers from my desk and glance at them, giving the impression that I do have other things to do.

"May we sit?" Alex asks as if he were hollering fire without diction or grammar.

"Please," I say as smoothly, trying to keep the wheels of communication running smoothly.

"Why this surprise visit?" I ask, emphasizing surprise to let them know they should have called for an appointment.

They are unfazed. They sit there as composed as occupation forces.

"Father Mike," Alex says in his usual pompous tone, "we had an emergency meeting of the Council"

"You've had a meeting without informing me, without my being there?" I ask letting my annoyance show like a flag waving in the breeze.

I am of the opinion that laypeople who make up parish councils and other parish committees have assumed the church triumphalism that had always been the trademark of the clergy. And still is in some segments of the 'renewed' church.

Now instead of Father knows best, it's the Council who knows everything about running a parish.

Too many who sit on Boards and Committees in the church bring with them the baggage of our culture's values. They don't base their observations and judgments on the gospel but on how it's done out there in the world.

"It was necessary that you not be present," Sarah says in her usual whiny, nasal tone.

"You see, Father Mike," now Alex sounds like his teaching a second grader, "there is this very important matter of the threat on your life. It has the people of the parish very, very upset."

Is this empathy? I think to myself without voicing it.

"Well," I say, "I'm touched by the concern of the people."

"It's more than concern," Sarah says, "it's worry."

"Worry?" I say.

"Yes," Alex responds as carefully as if he were picking his way through land mines, "with this assassin out to get you … well, we thought what if he should decide to ki … shoot you when you are with a gathering of parishioners."

"There is the possibility that many parishioners could be wounded or …" Sarah stopped, apparently unable to say the word, killed.

So I said it for her. "Killed?" I ask.

"Yes," she says softly and lowers her eyes.

"So you are not really concerned about my welfare," I say with an audible sigh.

"Oh," Alex chimes in, "we are concerned. We don't want anything to happen to you."

"That's why," Sarah adds, "we decided it would be a good idea if you took a leave of absence or a sabbatical."

"And if I'm not shot and killed, I could return as pastor?" Now I feel as though I'm playing a game with these two. "How long would I have to wait before I could return?"

Obviously this hadn't come up at the Council meeting. They both sit there as silent as the inside of a hearse.

"How will we know, what will be the indicator that the threat to my life is no longer in play?"

Again silence.

"Now," I say, this time I sound like the teacher trying to explain the rules of classroom procedure to two recalcitrant students, "let's talk about proper procedure.

"First, the Parish Council should not meet without the pastor's say-so.

"Secondly, the Parish Council has no authority to even suggest that a pastor take a leave of absence, never mind dictate it.

"Thirdly, only the Cardinal can make such a suggestion. And that's all it would be, a suggestion not a command under obedience.

"Fourthly, the Cardinal did make such a suggestion and I refused.

"Finally, whenever there is a gathering, I will make certain that I am standing off by myself so that the assassin can have a clear shot at me.

"Now if you'll excuse me, I have business to attend to. Good day."

I know that I am as abrupt as an irascible mountain man. But that's exactly the image and message I want to give.

"Oh, by the way," I call after them, "another procedure, and so you know who's in charge, if you ever hold a secret meeting again, I will disband the present Council and hold elections for a new one, present members not eligible to be candidates."

I surely would like to eavesdrop on the telephone conversations that would take place later on that night.

70

So much for concern about the pastor's welfare, not to mention his safety.

I go up to my room. I sit down and do some meditating.

I open the gospel story to Jesus' entering the synagogue.

Jesus is no longer teaching on an out-of-the-way hillside but sits down now to teach in a synagogue as out in the open as the birds of the air or the lilies of the field. All eyes are fixed on him with the same intensity as the Magi had in following the guiding star.

He has come to Nazareth carried on the waves of enthusiastic amazement and high esteem by all who had heard him.

Unlike his cousin John who calls people back to the old law, Jesus comes to make all things new.

To make all things new, Jesus knows he has to discard the old wineskins that would do nothing but burst under the pressure of the fresh wine of his teachings.

To make certain that the fruit he is planting will be an abundant harvest, Jesus shows loving concern for all people by rooting out the weeds of Jewish prejudice and hatred against the Gentiles.

So Jesus proclaims that God's loving concern is all inclusive.

The people protest in cries that get louder and louder with the increased mass hysteria. Our God, the God of the Chosen People, will never extend salvation to those Roman pagans who worship as many gods as there are soldiers in a regiment. He will never offer his blessings to those Samaritans who worship on Mount Gerizim instead of in the holy city of Jerusalem as we do.

What I need, it seems to me, perhaps desperately need, to ask myself, How open is my loving concern for others? Like the Chairman and Chairwoman of my parish council. Will I let the door of my heart stand open to receive people as they are not as I think they should be? Or will I allow my judgmentalism slam the door of my heart shut?

I am reading Kathleen Norris' book, _The Cloister Walk_. She says that we need a focused love to grow into the kind of openness we need if we are going to see and hear each other in a world torn apart by our differences

For example, do we see those who would rather live off the dole of society than be involved in productive work as members with us of the same community? Or do we just discount them as being lazy or stupid? Do we truly appreciate differences among people according to skin color or ethnic background? Do we encourage rather than tolerate these differences? Can I apply this to my Chairman and Chairwoman?

If I would meet a disoriented drug addict on the street would I call the police or a relief agency – or would I just be a passerby like the high priest and the Levite who hurried past the beaten and robbed man dying in the wayside ditch?

Do we ignore the malnutrition and starvation of a Third World country as we listen to the sounds of a lawn being watered or inhale the smell a backyard cookout?

Are we involved in feeding the hungry or clothing the naked or have we trivialized our religion, claiming that all we must do is save our own souls?

How concerned are we about the people around us who are in need? Whether their needs are material or emotional or psychological or relational or spiritual.

Does the door of my heartfelt loving concern stand wide open to all or is there just a small opening for a chosen few?

I certainly still have a lot of work to do. Once again, it's a case of that's the gospel, we're talking about real life.

Tragically, the main concern good Catholics show is for themselves. For the people who might be shot and killed by standing in a group around me.

God, give me courage and perseverance.

71

Don Giovanni gathers his henchmen around him.

"Here's what I want youse to do," he says in the idiom they will understand.

"Now pay strict attention. Because if youse mess up, youse will be meeting your God sooner than youse expected.

"I'm sendin' these photos and crib sheet to the mail box Charon says. It's box 242213 at the main post office in da city.

"I figure Charon's gonna pick the stuff up.

"Now here's my plan. Two of youse will camp out in that post office and wait for Charon to show up. Youse can arrange a schedule as to how many will be needed to substitute for one anutter. Make it six hour turns. I want to see the schedule."

"What do youse want us to do onct we spot Charon? Petey the Weasel asks.

"Take him," the Don answers in an annoyed way to indicate that he's telling them the obvious.

"Take him and bring him here," the Don commands.

"Should we have backup?" Andrew the Duckhead asks.

"If the two in the post office do what they should, I don't see no reason for backup," the Don answers curtly.

"Won't the people working in the post office get suspicious as to why we are there for six hours at a time?" This from Nicky the Nose.

"It's a public place. Nobuddy can tell youse to leave." Now the Don seems to be enjoying this repartee.

"When do youse want us to start?" Joe the Jock asks.

"Get that schedule to me right away and then start as soon as I give my okay," the Don uses his most sinister smile.

"We can spend a lot of hours –even days – hanging around that post office," Nicky the Nose complains.

"He gives us three to five days," the Don growls. "If that's too much for you, go find another place to hang your jock.

"No ... no, it's okay," Nicky the Nose stammers.

"What if dis ... dis Charon resists?" Joe the Jock asks.

"Then take him out, for God's sake," the Don bellows. "You want I should do it myself? Why do I have youse guys hanging around?"

The Don's henchmen began to realize that this meeting is over.

"And God help you if youse fail me," the Don slams a heavy period at the end of the meeting.

72

It seems to me that sadness follows us like a dark cloud. It envelops us like a black shroud.

I think of funerals I've had for babies and little children and teens who died in an accident. Death is always sad but in these cases sadness clings to me like the smell of a skunk.

And so this evening there is another tragic sadness that attacks me like fired bazooka.

The police come to my door.

They ask me if I am Father Mike. I say, "Yes."

They say, "There's been a murder and we found your card on the victim's body."

I say, "Do you know who the victim is?"

They say, "We are hoping you can identify him for us."

So I go with the police several long blocks from the rectory, followed by my bodyguards.

Laying there in the mud is the body of Logan Helfry, the future concert pianist.

A group of people are already gathered. There is a growing murmur of anger among them.

My heart, I swear, stops for three seconds. Tears well up in my eyes. I lean down and give Logan conditional absolution, although I firmly believe he's in heaven accompanying the angels in their songs of praise.

I study Logan's body, without disturbing anything, and see a knife wound right below his heart and a number of other stab wounds all around.

Who? Why?

I remember Logan telling me how he is taunted because he prefers the piano to basketball since he is so tall.

Could this be the reason?

How could it be?

"It's Logan Helfry, my parishioner," I say to the police.

The police say, "Thank you, Father Mike, there's no reason to remain here. We'll drive you home."

Home? Where is my home? Isn't it right here? But I go with one of the officers who drives me back to the rectory.

73

The next morning, bright and early, after I celebrate a distracted Mass, I call in Scuds, my reliable informant.

Of course, Scuds knows about the murder of Logan.

"My condolences," he says, "I knows he was close to youse."

"Scuds," I say to him, "I'm giving you a job that's the most important in your entire life."

"And what's that?" he says back to me.

"I want you to find out for me who killed Logan."

"That's a pretty big job," he says.

I know he's into bargaining.

"What do you need, Scuds?" I ask him.

"Well, I was thinkin' I need a new coat … and shoes."

"How much?" I ask.

"Oh, fifty dollars should do it," he says.

Even though I have the money in desk drawer, I leave the office and get the money out of my pocket. You can never be too careful.

Two days later, Scuds shows up with a young girl. He introduces her as Maisie.

I say, "Hello, Maisie."

She doesn't respond. She seems petulant. She keeps looking around as if trying to find a way to escape.

Scuds says, "Maisie here has some info that youse may be looking for, Fadder."

I say, "Won't you sit down Maisie? You'll be more comfortable." To Scuds I say,

"Would you leave us alone, please, Scuds?

Scuds looks disappointed, even annoyed, but he does step out. I figure with his ear to the closed door.

74

"Where do you live, Maisie?" I ask gently, hoping to break the ice and put her at ease.

"Nowhere," she says with what appears to be peevishly defensive.

"Are your parents living?" I ask with almost strained patience. It's obvious to me that this is not going to be chit-chat.

"I guess so," she answers me now with a show of annoyance.

Suddenly it dawned on me that perhaps she has been subject to police grilling and this is the reason for her sulfurous resentment.

"Maisie," I say to her, "I'm not here to accuse you of anything. I need your help."

"Help?" she mimics.

"Yes, I have a good friend. He's been killed and I'm looking for any help I can get to find out who killed him."

"Youse talkin' 'bout Logan?" She seems to have relaxed a bit when she found out I am not threatening her.

"Yes," I say most gently. "I'm talking about Logan."

"What's you askin' me fer?" she asks, defenses up like a missile shield.

"Look, Maisie, I know you know. All I want you to do is to give me a name. I promise you no harm will come to you."

I'm thinking of Forrow Haven. It's as good a safe house as any the Government department could supply. And it's under the surveillance of the Don.

There Maisie would not only be safe, but she would have the opportunity to turn her life around.

I explain Forrow Haven to Maisie, filling her in on all the details of the Haven. She sits there registering nothing but listening.

"Youse means youse could get me inta a place like that?" she asks, neither showing enthusiasm nor cynicism.

"I most definitely can," I say back to her in my most persuasive voice.

"Wellll," she drags the word out as if trying to tease me, "Heymond didn't do it."

She really was stretching my patience, as I prayed she would come through.

"Heymond was just standin' there."

"Were you standing there too?" I asked gently.

"Not really. I was standin' about a block aways. But there was this here street light. I could see it all goin' down."

"And …?" I say, hoping I would get the name.

"And," she says, if playing a game or trying to see how long I'd be patient, so if I lost my patience, she'd have reason to bolt, never giving me the name.

Then as quietly as a nun in prayer she says, "It was Tayshun and Rashid."

They killed Logan?" I asked her.

"No, they knock Logan down and start kickin' him. Then Tayshun, he takes out a knife and starts to stab Logan. Logan's screaming. Rashid, he yells at Tayshun to stop, but Tayshun, he keeps stabbin' Logan.

"Heymond, he just keeps standin' there watchin'

"Then the tree of them runs off, down the alley. I didn't do nothin' neither.

"Okay," I say, "thank you, Maisie. You are very helpful."

"Youse ain't gonna tell 'em, are youse?" she whines, almost shivering.

"I promise you I will not tell them," I tell her as sincerely as a bridegroom making his marriage vow. "Now I want to take you to Forrow Haven. Are you willing to go?"

"Yeah, I guess so."

I call Mavis Sullivan, who's doing a wonderful job learning the ins and outs of Forrow Haven and caring for the women there.

She hasn't taken over yet. She's still working at Octogenics full time as Mosley's Executive Assistant.

She spends her evenings at Forrow Haven, getting to know the ladies, winning their trust and helping Christine Joyce in the transition.

"Mavis," I say, it's Father Mike. I have someone I'd like to bring over. Is that all right?"

With her usual rush of enthusiasm she almost bellows, "Bring her right over, Father Mike. I'll be waiting for you both."

75

I get Maisie settled in. She looks like she's being led to a prison cell, but Mavis hugs her and cradles her. When I'm leaving I notice tears in Maisie's eyes. I pray they're tears of relief and joy. Who knows?

When I get back to the rectory, somehow I feel like *I* am going into a cell. Father Ambrose "Skip" Hecken, my recent "roomy," is waiting for me.

"Hi," I say to him. He looks at me and says, "You look beat."

"I am, sort of," I say to him.

"Mike," he says to me, "you've got to slow down. You have this huge parish to run and then you get so involved in extra curricular activities …" His voice fades off as though he presumes that I know exactly what he is saying.

"Then," Skip continues, "there's this Charon thing, following you like a black cloud. That's enough stress to buckle the most courageous."

"I guess so," I mutter, not feeling up to this conversation.

"What kind of a name is Charon anyway?" Skip asks obviously trying to change the subject.

"I looked it up on Google," I say. "Charon, in Greek mythology, is the ferryman of the dead. The souls of the deceased are brought to him by Hermes, and Charon ferries them across the river ... The river Acheron not the Styx as sometimes stated."

"So our Charon," Skip follows up, "is the one who carries dead people across the river by assassinating them."

"That's it," I say, guessing more than asserting a fact.

"That's interesting," Skip says.

"What's interesting?" I ask not really interested in the answer.

"You have all these books but you use Google."

Now he's talking about my books. It's like a verbal kaleidoscope.

"You're one up on me," Skip says. "I'm computer illiterate and I don't read many books."

I say, "I'm an autodidact. For me the studies we endured in seminary were a boring waste. I started teaching myself when, as a young priest, I began to teach children in high school. I had to learn before I could teach with any competency."

"So," Skip says, "you're self taught."

"You could say that," I say back to him.

"Well," Skip says, "for me books are too systematic, too absolute. Books aren't like life – disarranged, unpredictable, shabby, loose-ended, mysterious, ecstatic and depressive, joyous and negating, more problems than solutions."

"Books," Skip continues (I am interested. I'm not sure if this is self-revelation or his attempt to distract me from all the problems I'm dealing with) "have a beginning, a middle, an end. But so does life. Life begins, it has a middle, but for the most part, is undecipherable and not as smooth or well laid out like in a book. Then an end that comes when you least expect it, even though you're preparing for it since the beginning."

With a book, you know when the end is coming.

Skips stops. I'm more than a little impressed with his insights. He's quite the man. I say, "We begin dying the moment we're born."

"Exactly! Let's have a drink. You look like you could use a stiff one."

Actually I am feeling quite refreshed. It's so good to have someone who understands.

We are getting along all right which is something. But now somehow I feel we are bonded. I think he feels the same way.

I whisper a prayer of thanks.

76

Next morning after Mass, I call Detective Alison Masconi.

"Hello, Detective," I say to her. "It's Father Mike."

"Yes, Father Mike. I recognize your melodious voice."

I imagine her smiling that pixy smile she has.

I fill her in on Maisie. She's all attention.

I give her the names of the three perps. She asks me to repeat them.

I also tell her the whole story that Maisie told me.

I say, "Not to tell you how to do your business but it seems to me that Heymond's the weak link. He's the onlooker. Perhaps a few well placed threats could bring him around."

"In the meantime," Alison says, "we'll pick up those two thugs. With what you told me about Logon Helfry, this is one of the most detestable crimes we've had around here in a long time."

"I couldn't agree more. The potential Logan has … had …" I could feel myself filling up. So I turn to a more practical matter.

"Alison," I say to her, "please don't use Maisie's name. The poor girl's plunged into a trauma. She fears that Tayshun could reach out to her even through prison bars."

"Trust me, Father Mike," Alison gives a short but reassuring laugh. "And I will put the screws to the shabby witness, Heymond."

A few days later, Alison calls me.

"We've rounded up all three of them, Father Mike," she says to me.

"Heymond spilt his guts like a stabbed pig. He's still crying like a banshee."

"And Tayshun?" I ask.

"The stupid kid still had his knife. We've sent it to the lab. I have no doubt we'll find a match."

"And Maisie?"

"With all the evidence we have we won't need her to testify," Alison says reassuringly.

I breathe a deep sigh of relief and I whisper a sincere prayer of thanks.

??

The next morning I'm coming over from Mass. Today is the feast of our patron, St. Ignatius Loyola.

There was a pretty decent group at Mass. It makes me feel what I'm doing is worthwhile.

I don't know if the people got the point of my homily.

I told them that in process thought, a saint is not just a model for us to imitate; rather a saint pours out into us his/her dominant power. It is up to us to open our own becoming to receive this dominant power.

For example, St Francis of Assisi's love of creation can be an active source of our concern and work for ecological preservation; but we must first be convinced of the need for our work to preserve and improve our environment and be willing to do this work.

Then our prayer to St. Francis becomes the channel through which his dominant power of his love for creation flows into us. This increases our process of becoming all God wants us to be.

When it comes to our own patron saint, St. Ignatius, his dominant power is perseverance.

After he dropped out of the army, he went back to school. All the other students were younger and he had great difficulty adjusting as well as learning.

Although it took him a long time to finish his studies, he stuck with it.

He persevered then and afterwards, when he found the order known as the Jesuits, he persevered in missionary work, fostered such glorious disciples as St. Francis Xavier. He poured his zealous perseverance into Francis and other disciples.

So too today our patron saint releases his power of perseverance into us. It's not so much our trying to match his zealous perseverance by imitation.

Rather it's accepting the zeal and perseverance he is offering us in response to our prayers to him.

It is a process in which his zeal and perseverance becomes our zeal and perseverance. But again we must be open to receiving and accepting his gift of zealous perseverance.

The same is true of St. Theresa of Avila's dominant power of mysticism. But we must want the mystical experience in order to open ourselves up to receive and accept her dominant power.

When we receive her dominant power we grow in the process of our becoming mystics.

Mystical experience itself is a process, going from fuller to fuller to fullest.

I hope my homily isn't so esoteric that it's incomprehensible. Oh well, let the Holy Spirit enlighten them. I try to do my part.

Standing in the pulpit, I realize there are many mystics sitting in front of me. Mysticism is usually thought of as an extraordinary experience.

But for the person who is aware of and filled with wonder at familiar things, like sunsets, flowers, bugs, children, picnics, bread and wine, mysticism is for ordinary people.

As Chesterton said, Stare at the familiar until it becomes unfamiliar.

Mysticism is for everyone, whether saints or sinners

78

Skip is sitting at the kitchen table eating cereal.

"Happy feast day I say to him."

"Right back at you," he says with that ferocious grin of his.

"Had a nice turn out for Mass," I say.

"Me too. About double the usual number for the 6:30," he sounds jubilant.

"You know," Skip says, "I was sitting here thinking about the beauty of the present day Eucharistic celebration like the one we had this morning."

I give him my full attention since he rarely shares what he is thinking and this sounds like a deep insight coming.

"You know what bothers me?"

"No, but I'm sure you're going to tell me." I laugh and he joins me.

"Well," he says, "it's amazing to me that forty years later there are those who still resent the changes of Vatican II."

I let him continue his thought without interrupting with my words of agreement.

(We used to have a coach in high school who would say, "I'm in agreeance with you").

"It's not just the liturgical changes, but all of the changes of that magnificently renewing Council," Skip continues.

"And they hide their resentment behind the change of the Mass into the vernacular.

"They say when the Mass was in Latin you could go anywhere in the world and the Mass was always the same. How many of them go anywhere in the world?

"I think they construct a defense system that even God's releasing and liberating grace can't get through to them.

"Oh, they're pious enough in a me-and-my-God kind of worship.

"What puzzles me is how they can kneel in church 'attending' a Latin Mass that objectifies their unadmitted resentment to the so-called 'new' Mass which has been around for forty years.

"As Flannery O'Connor said, 'Grace is not always gentle.' At times, it seems to me, grace has to be rough, even tumultuous, to break open people's defenses.

"Sometimes grace has to blast people out of their nostalgic ruts so that they can finally respond to the call of Jesus who makes all things new.

"We either adapt to change or we're left behind and some people would be satisfied to stay in the eternal behind."

Skip paused and took a gulp of his coffee which I assume was cold.

I am absolutely overwhelmed with his insights. And this is the guy who said he doesn't read much, quoting Flannery O'Connor. She must be blushing around the golden throne.

Skip and I are definitely soul mates. I feel so close to him.

All I could say is, "You're right on, Skip."

That seems to be satisfaction enough for him.

Later I am thinking that in process thought change is the essence of reality. Not substance. Not something.

The basic elements in process thought are flexibility, evolution, growing and developing.

Reality is fluid like river moving forward.

And that's the way I look at the changes in the Mass.

I must say that I am deeply impressed with Skip's outlook. He may not be a scholar in the traditional meaning of that term, but his observations are as astute as any scholar I'm familiar with.

I'm so fortunate to have him as a "roomy." May God keep him close to his heart.

Imagine, quoting Flannery O'Connor!

79

The trial of the three boys who killed Logan Helfry is short and swift.

I don't go to the trial. I just don't want to hear the gruesome details of Logan's death. I'm still mourning him.

Such talent. So unassuming. I think he truly lived St. Paul's question, "What do you have that you have not received?"

Logan realized that everything he had, everything he was, came as a precious gift from God.

He won't be canonized, but he truly lived his faith. His faith pulsed through him like his bloodstream.

As long as I live, as long as I pray, I'll never understand this kind of evil.

Time and again I try to probe the problem of evil as so many before me.

One idea I have is that there is evil in the world because believers don't tap into the overwhelming goodness which God is constantly offering us.

I guess it's the old bromide, Evil triumphs when good people do nothing.

We have God's power within us, but how conscious are we of this power? How often do we seize and use this power?

Don't we sink into hopelessness as if it's quicksand?

And when we pray, isn't it like asking God to do it all for us? Expecting God to wave a magic wand and make everything nice?

In the novel, *Pillars of Fire*, the abbot says, "Pray for miracles, but plant potatoes."

When will we understand that our cooperative efforts are essential? It's with our cooperative efforts that we do tap into the power God is forever offering us.

Switching slides, I realize that I must get out into my parish more, be more visible, strive to be more influential.

Sometimes I wonder if my involvement in helping to solve murders and other felonies is taking away from my presence as pastor.

Anyway, Rashid and Heymond were sentenced to five to twenty-five years.

Tayshun, who did the actual killing, was sentence to life in prison without the possibility of parole.

Justice is done.

I plan to visit these boys within the week. After I spend time with Logan's mother. A wonderful woman who had such ecstatic dreams for her son. Now a crushed bundle of a frozen heart and sterilized soul. Hopelessness punctuating her every sob.

Perhaps I can elicit remorse for the boys' sin.

Being punished by civil law does not necessarily evoke sorrow for sin. That's the obligation of religion.

I don't intend to force them. At the same time, I'm not going feed them spiritual pabulum.

I guess you could call it tough love. I pray it works.

Only Jesus can touch their hearts. So I'm going to spend time in prayer before visiting them.

Meanwhile I am still mourning the death of Logan.

Being a pastor has its downsides.

80

Mavis Sullivan takes a deep breath as she stands outside the headquarters of Bradford and Bradford.

She still has all her keys.

She left Bradford the day after the day she was offered the job and Forrow Haven. She never formally resigned. So, for all intents and purposes, she is still the personal -- slave. Besides, she had not yet formally begun her work at Forrow Haven.

Now she would use her keys. Would she ever!

She finally exhales a gust of breath and opens the door to the empire.

The night guard is seated behind the ornate counter. Anything to impress.

Mavis recognizes him from his daytime duty.

"Hi, Sam," Mavis greets him cheerily.

"Good evening, Mavis. Haven't seen you for a while."

Good, Mavis thinks, he doesn't know I left.

"Off to the Bahamas for a well-earned vacation," Mavis gives her best professional smile.

"You missed all the excitement," Sam says.

"Oh, I heard all about it, Sam. Had to cut my time by ten days."

"Guess you've seen the Boss, Mr. Mosley."

"Yeah, he sent for me personally," Mavis is still smiling.

"In fact, he's sent me to pick up some papers and tapes for him. You know, a workaholic and such," she says as glibly as if making a smartaleck remark about another co-worker.

"Okay, Mavis. Just sign in here."

Mavis is prepared for this. If someone checks this and finds she had returned, especially at night, she would already have all the evidence needed. So who cares? The list is rarely, if ever, checked.

She can't be prosecuted for breaking and entering. After all, she has keys. She never formally quit. No one ever told her to turn them in. As far as others are concerned, she may be hiding out for fear of being accused of being in collusion with Mosley. There's a chance of being caught, but it will probably never materialize.

"Well, Sam, I better get going. Don't want to keep the Boss waiting. You know how he gets," Mavis says as she finished signing her name which she did with a bit of unusual flourish, hoping to disguise her signature.

"Okay, Mavis. Take care."

Even if Sam checks her out rummaging through Mosley's office, he'll just see her doing what she told him she was going to do.

31

Mavis inserts the key into Mosley's private office and opens the door. At first, slowly, then she just throws open the door.

Should she use her flashlight? No. If Sam might look in, she should be acting the part of legitimately gathering Mosley's documents and tapes.

She has Father Mike's list.

But she wants to gather even more than what's on the list. Her way of showing her disgust with, her loathing of her "former" boss.

Mavis uses her keys to open doors in the cabinets that fill two walls in Mosley's office. Now she uses her flashlight to examine various papers. Some she shoves back into the shelves, others she jams into her bag.

Then she goes to Mosley's computer.

Many times Mosley ordered her to go into his computer and print out something he needed. So she has no trouble getting in.

She finds innumerable records of phone calls.

Why wouldn't he have deleted these? She wonders.

Because he's a megalomaniac. Because he was convinced he was above all laws.

Mavis prints out all the numbers of the phone calls and thrusts them into her bag.

She goes through a myriad of transactions.

Without reading them closely, she realizes what a felon Mosley is.

She prints these out even though Father Mike didn't have them on his list.

By now she's wondering if Sam is watching her. Who cares? She's found a gold mine here. More accurately, a cesspool.

Mavis returns things to their proper place just in case one of Mosley's henchmen checks out his office. If he sees things in order, he'll just take a momentary glance and leave.

Mavis takes the express elevator down.

"Goodnight, Sam," she says.

"Boy, you had a lot to get, didn't you?" Sam says.

"The Boss might as well have sent me into a jungle," Mavis laughs.

Mavis starts for the door.

"Oh, Mavis," Sam calls out.

Mavis freezes in her spot. What now? Does Sam want to go through my bag? No, he wouldn't understand what was in it.

She slowly turns and gives that alluring smile she used so often in her previous occupation.

"Please ... tell the Boss I send my personal regards."

"I sure will, Sam." Like Mosley would ever know who Sam is.

Mavis goes through the door which automatically locks behind her. She stands with her back up against the wall of the building, on the verge of hyperventilating, trying to grasp her breath and stop shaking.

Just then a car pulls up.

"Come on, Mavis," Father Mike calls out. "We'll pick up your car in the early morning."

Mavis throws her bag in the back of the car, gets in beside Father Mike.

"I need one big drink," she sort of giggles.

32

It's Monday and Charon is checking his schedule.

He has five days until he picks up the assignment from the Don.

But first he has this huge job to do.

According to the plan, this first job must be done on Wednesday.

He's getting two million down and three million after it's done. It's the largest sum he ever asked for and got, no questions asked.

The money is to be sent as usual to his Swiss bank account.

Once again his clients would pay the remainder or they would be looking down the barrel of his rifle. They know this. Word gets around.

Charon picks up the rationale for the job. Usually he doesn't read them. He asks for them so his clients have to face up to what he read about: their Shadow Self – that part of themselves so despicable that they don't even want to admit it exists.

This time it's different.

After all, taking out the Vice President of the United States of America deserves some explanation.

The rationale begins:

It is common knowledge that the present occupant of the White House is not the brightest crayon in the box. But the President is cunningly ruthless. And Shayne knows exactly how to tap into the President's harsh, opportunistic side.

Charon pauses. Why is the spelling of the Vice President's name pronounced Shane?

Charon continues to read: As a result, the President leans absolutely on his Vice President, Rick Shayne, like a little boy holding onto his daddy's hand.

We have discovered through stringent and depthful research that Rich Shayne desperately wants to be President so much so that he intends to challenge his own President when the President runs for a second term.

While he has a right to do so, he continues to publicly profess total loyalty to his President.

Rick Shayne intends to announce his intention to run for President on Wednesday Sept 17 this year.

Again through scrupulous research we have found Rick Shayne to be the most treasonable person to hold this position.

There is no doubt that the President is a puppet and the Vice President is the puppet master.

It was Rick Shayne who persuaded the President to invade the sovereign nation of Columbia, South America under the pretext that Columbia was plotting a sneak attack against the United States of America.

This war has dragged on during the entire first term of the President, fueled by the gushy euphoric, glamorized hypertense oratory of the Vice President.

Over 5,000 military personnel have been killed. Over 37,000 wounded. And there is no light at the end of the tunnel.

The Vice President is constantly playing the fear card, keeping the ordinary people frozen in dread. The people are so paralyzed in fear that they don't even want to be led. And so the Vice President just ignores them.

The Vice President has anointed himself as the all knowing guru. Behind the scenes, he is absolutely convinced that he can brainwash the people into believing that he is their savior, their flawless leader doing everything for their good, their comfort and their security while the people have no idea that their freedoms are being siphoned off unnoticeable drop by unnoticeable drop.

Rick Shayne is nothing short of being, in effect, a tyrant. He wears a velvet glove to cover his steel fist.

The Vice President depends, as no other elected official ever has, on the citizens of our great country being a "nation of sheep."

But he is not the shepherd. He is a hired hand.

Charon pauses again. This is good writing, he thought. Even a reference to a gospel parable.

These clients are not only wealthy, but highly intelligent, provided they didn't get a "hired hand" to write this rationale. Anyway they had to be intelligent enough to sign off on it.

83

Charon reads on:

With Shayne, there are still lingering questions about capacity, motive, or malice. Over the past four years, as the country has spiraled into military misadventure, fiscal madness, and environmental meltdown, the Vice President has not merely been wrong about the issues; he has been duplicitous, deceitful, and deliberately destructive to American democracy.

These things can no longer be denied by rational minds: that as the war in Columbia devolved into occupation, the Vice President again sabotaged the democratic system, developing back channels into the Coalition Provisional Authority, a body under his authority, to remove some of the most effective staff and replace them with his own loyal supplicants - undercutting America's best effort at war in order to expand his own power;

In his domestic capacity, the Vice President has been equally reckless with the trust of his office, converting the Vice Presidency into a de facto prime ministership, even a co-presidency, conducting secret meetings with secret policy boards to determine national policy and then refusing to share the details of those meetings with the other branches of government and perhaps with the President himself.

Rick Shayne is presiding over crony capitalism.

Crony capitalism is the practice of government supporting specific companies or industries for favorable treatment in legislation, government grants, legal permits and beneficial tax laws.

This includes the company with which the Vice President has closest ties: Bradford and Bradford Octogenics.

The concepts of open competition and free markets do not apply, because government actively intervenes to assist privileged corporations. In crony capitalism, there is a close relationship between government and corporations, and their actions towards each other are mutually financially beneficial. National laws and regulations are enacted that provide special permission for particular companies for acquisitions, mergers, real estate transactions and tax benefits.

The *quid pro quo* for Republican and Democratic politicians are campaign donations, future jobs for themselves or relatives, and are disguised or hidden perks in exchange for favorable legislation for privileged organizations. Crony democracy occurs when crony capitalism merges with democracy, with major players becoming interchangeable with the lobbying promoting it.

34

Charon puts down the document and breathes an audible WOW! This is totally science fiction. This is totally unbelievable. But apparently true enough to have the Vice President assassinated.

Charon continues reading:

We have from an indisputable source that Vice President, Rick Shayne, has repeatedly asserted his office is not a part of the executive branch of the U.S. government, and therefore not bound by a presidential order governing the protection of classified information by government agencies.

Bill Sanson, head of the government's Information Security Oversight Office (ISOO), told Media outlets that Shayne's office has refused to provide details regarding classified documents or submit to a routine inspection as required by Presidential order. In fact, the Vice President has tried to get rid of Sanson's office.

Rick Shayne single-handedly politicized the Justice Department, using the U. S. Attorney as an arm of the Administration.

There can be no doubt that this man, Rick Shayne, is guilty of obstruction, malice of forethought, perjury and treason.

And here he is, not only the Vice President, but a man who intends to run for the Presidency of the United States of America.

There can be no doubt that Rick Shayne is an empire builder. A man who wants to be the global emperor. But first he must become President.

So on Wednesday September 17th, in the ballroom of the Watergate Hotel, he will announce his intention of running against his own party's President as well as whoever is nominated from the other party.

Noted psychiatrists, in off the record statement, claim that Rick Shayne is a schizophrenic megalomaniac. That if he is elected to the presidency, he will become a unfettered dictator and bring down the democratic government of the U. S. as no one has ever imagined it could be done.

Rick Shayne is suave, charismatic, soigné, persuasive, at times glamorous.

We are convinced that he could easily be elected President.

This is why we have chosen the radical approach of hiring your services.

We are willing to pay five million dollars: two now, three afterward. Believe us when we say you are doing your country a great service.

Charon sneered at this last sentence. Why don't these million or billionaires just pour money into a campaign against the Vice President.

That would be more democratic than having him iced.

Oh well, mine is neither to puzzle or ponder.

35

Charon has everything planned.

He reserved a room in the Howard Johnson's across the street from the Watergate.

The room has a full view of the entrance of the Watergate.

Ironic, Charon thinks, the place that caused the downfall of one President will be the place to end the plans of a wannabe President.

He has his long distance sniper rifle which he used constantly when he was in Special Ops where he spent four years. He was the best sniper in the unit. Still is. It is a Marine M40 sniper rifle used to assure accuracy and placement of shots at great distances.

Charon sends his rifle ahead. No one checks the luggage except carry-ons.

Charon flies from Chicago to Washington, D.C. He picks up his rifle, hires a car and drives to his hotel.

"Yes, Mr. Quigley, we have your reservation," the desk manager smiled pleasantly, almost lyrically.

Charon pays for one night with cash.

36

Charon carries his regular looking suitcase in which his broken down rifle was placed with great care.

He enters his room, checks it out, pulls the drapes closed except for the one in the middle.

He opens his suitcase and begins to put his M40 sniper rifle together.

He goes to the window and quietly cuts a small hole through the window with the skill of a surgeon.

He sits down by the window, places his rifle on his knees and looks out.

This work is not for the impatient. He waits as if watching the news on the TV.

The Vice President is due at the Watergate at noon. It is now 11:23 AM. Most likely the VP will be fashionably late.

It doesn't matter. He has all the time he needs.

As Charon continues to sit there, he begins to feel something. This is as unusual as the warmth of the sun on a cold winter evening.

Usually he never feels anything. Usually he is as empty as boredom.

Charon goes deep within himself, trying to discover what it is he's feeling.

Yes, he thought, he is feeling pleasure.

This man, this pretender to the throne of presidential power, this hypocritical, devious, blatant crook deserves to be eliminated.

Suddenly he realizes he has to repress this feeling.

He isn't a legend because he does his work based on fleeting feelings or penetrating, soul-searching thoughts.

37

Gradually, Charon hears the sirens in the distance.

He places his rifle's nose through the small hole he made in the window.

The barrel of his rifle was painted black so as to keep his gun from glimmering in any sunshine.

He picks out a point where he thinks the Vice President might stand after he gets out of the car or at least some place near that spot.

There are three cars in front of the black stretch limousine and four behind.

Quite a show of prestige Charon smiled.

As he expects, Charon has guessed the exact spot where Rick Shayne is standing and greeting swooning admirers.

He placed his M40 tightly against his shoulder and squinted through his telescope.

The Vice President's head was in full view. But his head was swerving back and forth as he greeted supporters who were as obviously thrilled as fans at a winning football game.

Charon had to wait with the patience of a crouched panther for the split moment when the VP's head came to a standstill.

Slowly, carefully he squeezed the trigger.

The back of Rick Shayne's head exploded. Screaming, scurrying, fainting, mob hysteria broke out as violently as a sudden earthquake.

Charon smiled at the irony. Shayne's head exploded like a smashed watermelon. A watermelon at the Watergate.

Slowly, deliberately he breaks down his M40 and places it carefully in his suitcase.

He walks toward the door. Then he turns back and drops a chewing gum wrapper on the floor under the window.

Won't they be surprised?

He walks casually down the hallway to the elevator. Takes it down to the garage. Gets into his rented car and drives to the airport.

Somewhere, Charon thinks, between the brilliant white light of truth and the bitter darkness of deceit is a place where many live in the shadows.

"The good old Shadow Self," he said aloud to himself with no emotion.

Oh well, now for the Don's contract. A measly quarter of a million dollars. Why does he even bother?

But then there is someone who has to meet his or her Maker. And he is the one who will take him or her across the river.

33

Mavis and I arrive at the rectory.

Mavis dumps all she gathered on the dinning room table. What a collection!

"I think we should call Detective Masconi," I say to Mavis.

"The sooner we turn this stuff over to some authority, the better I'll feel," she says back to me.

"How about that drink first?" I ask her.

"Bless you, Father," she smiles her gorgeous smile.

I pour her a dry Martini. She takes a generous gulp, exhales and says "Ahh, does that ever hit the spot!"

I make myself my usual Manhattan, Windsor Canadian with sweet Vermouth and cherry juice. Unlike Mavis I sip my drink. Unlike Mavis I didn't go through the debilitating tension of raiding Mosley's office.

I put a call in to Alison Masconi. Get her voice mail. I leave a message with the word, urgent.

"We'll just have to wait," I say to Mavis.

I turn on the TV and we watch the news. We're shocked.

It's all about the Vice President being assassinated as he was going into the Watergate ballroom to deliver and "important" message.

One anchor, a sour-looking older man, wearing an obvious wig, speculates that Rick Shayne was probably going to announce his run for the presidency.

"If so," he says, "someone or some group did not want him to run."

"The city, the nation is in an uproar," the other anchor, a fresh looking pretty young woman, reported. "Vice President Shayne was the poster boy for the political world. Smooth, likeable, articulate to the point of eloquence.

"The President has yet to make a statement. He's probably in a state of shock," she opines.

"Wonder if it's shock over his assassination or that his own Vice President intended to run against him," the man all but sneered.

"We won't know till the Pres makes his statement, will we?" the pretty young woman knitted her brow either in sincere seriousness or in an attempt to counteract her co-worker's flippancy.

"Charon!" I say out loud to no one in particular.

The male anchor continued, picking up on his co-anchor's solemnity.

"The FBI are claiming that the assassination was perpetrated by the international assassin, Charon. They found his telltale gum wrapper in the room in the hotel across from the Watergate."

"Of course," he continued, "it could always be a copycat."

He smirked again as if he had just solved the whole matter with the swiftness of Sherlock Holmes.

"My God," I breathed to Mavis.

I hate to admit it, but I think I am more upset at being Charon's target than the Vice President's murder.

39

In the Oval Office, the President sits at his desk, surrounded by his closest advisers.

The President looks haggard. His full head of hair was tangled from running his hand through it. His ruggedly handsome face was pale and drawn.

"He really was planning to run against me, wasn't he?" the President almost murmured in a threatening, defensive, hostile tone.

"It certainly seems that way," his chief adviser, a chubby, bald man, said. "I got it from his boy that he was going to announce at the Watergate."

"I guess we'll have to fly the flag at half mast," the President sounded bitter. "The symbol should be his plummeting down into hell."

"We'll have to figure out who will take his place," the President said with no particular interest. "Karl, get me a list. I want to have the name of the Shayne's replacement when I speak my heartfelt sorrow over that damnable Judas's unwarranted murder."

"I'll have it to you by two this afternoon," Karl sounded as enthusiastic as if the President has just put him in charge of a presidential party.

"What about this Charon?" The President asks with a prepackaged indifference from his protective pedestal.

"We've begun a nation-wide search for him," the weasel-looking head of Justice announced with do-gooder vanity.

"How are you going to find him?" Karl sneers. "Nobody knows what he looks like."

The Weasel just sits there in the silence of Zechariah struck dumb by an angel or in Karl's case, a devil.

"Who cares?" the President spoke menacingly. "Just announce a nation-wide search. Every transportation area watched. Make it appear that Charon is enemy number one."

"Frankly, if we could capture him, I'd like to pin a medal on him. Actually," the President smiles with arrogant impiety, "we will use Shayne's horrible demise as a springboard into the coming election. It should be a fait-accompli now."

The President sits back and lowers his head. Everyone in the office knows it's time to leave. Everyone knows the mind of their leader.

"Karl," the President calls after him as he was leaving, "get Frank, my speech writer, in here. I have to come up with some preposterous euphemisms wrapped in soul-searching sorrow and ingratiating believability."

Karl smiled. The Boss is already on the rose-covered path to this speech. "Yes, Sir, right away."

90

The mourning over the death of the Vice President's assassination mirrors that of the universal grief over John F. Kennedy's assassination.

Crowds muddle in the streets. Gathering in stunned silence, except for those who are openly crying as though members of Shayne's immediate family.

Like the time of JFK's assassination, families huddle around their television sets, waiting, watching, searching for any scrap of information about the assassination.

Still there is not a single word about who shot the Vice President or what the establishment is doing to track down the killer.

So far, there isn't a statement from the President. Of course, the people are not shocked at this fact, the President being who he is.

If nothing else, Rick Shayne was a charismatic leader. There were many who wanted him to be their President.

Even though he fostered and actually was the force of starting the war on Columbia, all behind the scenes, Shayne is now announcing how he will bring this war to an end as surely as Christmas ends like a blown fuse.

The current President is such a failure, such a stupid man that the citizens are fed up with the whole political establishment.

People keep asking one another, "How could he ever want to run for a second term?"

Rick Shayne was their hope for a new path through the jungle of the political morass that had enveloped the nation for the last four years.

91

In a plush den, six men sit around sipping brandy and smoking Cuban cigars. Each one is a multibillionaire. They are the older generation. Men of power who are used to being the movers and shakers behind the scenes like plotting and putting into effect the assassination of the Vice President.

Real power is what is done behind the scenes.

Despite all the excuses they proffered for Shayne's execution, Shayne was a populist who would run on a platform of challenging and stripping the wealthy of their complacent, comfortable lives in order to bathe the middle class and the poor in luxury.

"Damn the middle class," one of the men scowls. "Who travels from one end of the country to the other to sit through a football game? That same middle class that whines like a beggar with a tin cup."

Even worse, Shayne was as steadfastly against outsourcing as a statue implanted in concrete. This, the six men had decided was as intolerable and unimaginable as their declaring bankruptcy. After all, outsourcing is a the huge trapdoor through which their increasing wealth clangs into their coffers.

Shayne had been cooperating with them. Then when he decided to run for President, he broke all connections with them. This cost them a great deal financially.

As a result, when Shayne was questioned about Mosley's conglomerate, he denied even knowing Mosley.

This seems to call into question all the reasons these men gave to Charon justifying the assassination of the Vice President.

Although the reasons they did give were right on target. They just didn't give all the reasons

"The question before us, gentlemen," one of the men speaks as solemnly as a Pope making an infallible statement, "can the assassination be traced back to us?"

"As far as Charon's clients are concerned," another man says, "we enjoy anonymity."

"I have heard," a third man speaks up in a voice shaking as though springing from fear, "that Charon finds out who his clients are and keeps a portfolio on them ... just in case ..." His voice trailed off.

"Then," gentlemen, the first man says, "we must rid ourselves of this freak, Charon."

"How?" a fourth man whined. "Hire another assassin and then be right back where we are?"

"Except," the first man counters, "who will care that an assassin has been taken out? We can even use the spin that the hated assassin of the beloved Vice President has been killed."

"Makes sense to me," the fifth man says.

The sixth man looks directly at the first man. "You'll take care of the details?"

"I will."

92

Detective Alison Masconi arrives minutes after I call her; or so it seems.

She does a quick survey of the evidence on the dining room table.

"Wow!" she explodes. "Boy, Mavis, you sure dumped Mosley's office."

Mavis doesn't say anything. She just stands there, but you could feel her pride on a job well done as if Alison were applauding.

Then Alison says, "I'd better call FBI agent, Syl Kerns."

She quick dials Sylvester Kerns.

"Syl," she says with the excitement of a school girl getting her first friendship ring from her boy friend, "you gotta come over to St. Ignatius' rectory ASAP. We have evidence here on Mosley that should put him in prison for the rest of his life."

She shuts her cell. "He says he's gonna call 'Law and Order' Tobin over at Securities and Exchange and they'll both be over here in a matter of minutes."

223

"Good," I say. "The sooner we turn this material over to the authorities, the better."

"Kerns and Tobin will think they have a gold mine or a pigsty, depending on their point of view," Alison says.

FBI agent Sylvester Kerns arrives first. Minutes behind him is Lawrence Oliver Tobin, a.k.a "Law and Order" Tobin.

I show them into the dinning room. "Gentlemen," I say, "here is all the evidence you need," as I sweep my arm over the table like a magician finishing one of his tricks.

They both started to rummage through the contents on the dinning room table. It's obvious that they are very impressed as if they were misers who had just found a pot of gold.

"We need to take this stuff and let our techies go through it," FBI Syl Kerns speaks just above a whisper as though he were in church.

"Okay," Law and Order says, "but you must keep me in the loop."

Then Law and Order asks, "I wonder if this stuff will stand up in court. Your lady here broke and entered, then stole all this material."

I say, "Actually she didn't break and enter. She hasn't started her new work at Forrow Haven. She is still Mosley's Executive Assistant. She has every right to enter his inner sanctum. As far as her taking these materials from Mosley's office, she has done this many times to put them in some kind of order."

"We'll just have to let a judge make this call," Syl says. "Frankly, I can't see a judge throwing all this out once he gets a look at it or hears it."

"Of course," Law and Order says, "Mosley will have the best legal representation in the nation. Hell! maybe in the whole world."

"We'll just have to keep our fingers crossed," Detective Alison says.

"And pray," I add as fervently as a mystic.

93

Charon flies into Chicago as composed as someone who has just finished a hearty meal.

He hires a cab and goes to a local bar. He gets out, then hires another cab which takes him to a theater. Then a third cab which finally takes him to the apartment building where his room is.

He gets out of that cab, walks around the block and goes into the building from the rear. He had a key made for an occasion like this.

"Can't be too careful," he says to himself with a satisfied smile as he enters his room.

Tomorrow, the fifth day, he'll visit the Post Office and pick up the Don's information, then work on that assignment.

He is anything but exhausted. In fact, as usual, he feels rejuvenated. He always does whenever an assignment is completed successfully.

He turns on the television.

It's exploding with news about the assassination of the beloved Vice President.

Charon sits down with a glass of bourbon in hand to watch the reports. If the people only knew how "beloved" he really was, he sneered.

"The whole nation's in mourning," the perky red headed anchor screwed up her face to make certain she was in sync with all the mourners.

"Yes," her elder statesman anchor with an obvious toupee echoed. "The President sounded heartbroken, didn't he?"

"Wasn't there a rumor," she twists her face into a pronounced question mark, "that Vice President Shayne was going to announce his campaign for President, running against the President?"

"I heard that," the statesman speaks as if he were an oracle, "but either that's a false rumor or the President didn't know about it."

"I doubt the President wouldn't know *that*," Perky exclaims as though she were saluting the flag.

"So," Statesman responds in a mature, measured tone, "that means the rumor was baseless … groundless." He likes using synonyms to bolster his commentary.

"Even though we haven't got verification," Perky says, "the rumor circulating is that the assassin is the infamous, world-known Charon."

"So," Statesman says almost in a conspiratorial tone, "this means that someone or some group or some political opponents are behind this assassination."

"That's certainly not a leap," Perky says as she flutters her eyes in admiration for her colleague.

"And that's it for tonight," Statesman states authoritatively as Perky joins in with a smiling goodbye.

94

Both of the Don's men, Squeaky and Clop, feel as bored as children playing the same game over and over for hours on end.

Squeaky is a slight little man, thin as a rail, but wiry. His face tells you he can spring into action on a moment's notice and be as vicious as a lion attacking its prey.

Clop is big and burly. He looks like a statue in a museum. His face tells you nothing. And you wonder if there is anything behind that face.

Their names are based on their voices.

Squeaky has a high-pitched, shrill voice like the cry of a mouse.

Clop has a hollow sound like a horse's hoof striking a pavement.

They're taking their turns standing around the main Post Office for four days. They're tired of being stared at.

At one point, the manager of the Post Office comes to them and asks if he can help them.

They remember what the Don told them: be nice, be pleasant. Don't give anyone a reason to call the cops.

"We're just waiting for an important package, Sir," Clop says as gently as a soothing mother, but the volume of his voice is still as terrifying as a barbarian coming over the Alps to invade Rome.

The manager somehow feels threatened. Yet there's nothing the two men are doing that would warrant calling the police. So he bows perfunctorily and goes back to his office.

Don's two men look at each other and smile. They feel a thrill between them like a spark of electricity at how they pulled it off.

At least this is a break in the boredom. In fact they are basking in their new-found profession as actors.

This is their last day.

95

On this, the fifth day, an old man enters the Post Office.

Squeaky and Clop hardly take notice.

Then Squeaky nudges Clop and points to the mail box.

"It's him," Squeaky whispers but his whisper is what you might expect: a squeak.

The old man at the mail box spins around with gun in hand.

Squeaky and Clop had their guns out already.

The old man fires a shot and Clop goes down, dead as a doornail as they say.

The people in the Post Office scream, some run for the door, others drop to the floor, yelling and bleating and praying.

The old man quickly turns his gun on Squeaky, but Squeaky gets a shot off and hits the old man in the left side.

Disrupted by the shot in the side, the old man's shot misses Squeaky's heart and hits him in the shoulder.

Like a deer, the old man springs out of the Post Office, roughly shoving aside the few who are trying to escape from the Post Office building.

Outside, Josh the Mush, waiting to take his turn in the Post Office, heard the shots inside. He is standing by the car, gun out and raised. He sees the old man running our of Post Office, but is too befuddled to realize who he is. Josh the Mush thinks it's another guy trying to get away.

The old man, seeing the gun, fires a shot on the run and hits Josh the Mush in the forehead.

The old man's down the street quicker than sudden streak lightning.

He's holding his left side, the blood as obvious as a rain storm.

96

After the FBI agent, Syl Kernes, reports back to Lawrence Oliver Tobin of the Securities and Exchange Commission, Tobin decides to report back to Father Mike who has been so instrumental in getting this evidence.

"We've got Mosley, Father Mike. In spades!"

"I'm so grateful for your call," I say back to him; "that's the best news I've heard in a long time."

"It looks like we can get Mosley in his manipulating Bradford and Bradford Octogenic Chemicals for corruption, theft, kickbacks, bribery as well as for fraud, market manipulation, bribery. blackmail, payoffs and insider trading, mail fraud, violation of Federal election laws," the usual totally composed Law and Order Tobin sounds breathless with the excitement of a swimmer who had just won the gold.

Law and Order continues: "we can convict him of 24 counts of grand larceny, conspiracy and securities fraud. His arrogance, I'm sure, will keep him from fleeing.

He built his empire from a 40 million dollar company to a 54 trillion dollar conglomerate.

He pocketed 1.3 trillion through the sale of company stocks off market and running hundreds of billions worth of personal expenses through interest free company loan programs."

"And, of course," I say, there is the hiring of an assassin …"

"Yes, of course," Law and Order says back to me. "And we have proof of Mosley hiring and paying Charon."

"Sounds like life without parole," I say.

"Life without parole," Law and Order concurs.

97

After I hung up from talking to Law and Order, I sat behind my desk, trying to puzzle why an individual would act like Mosley.

Mosley had built his company into a world-wide empire.

Why was he obsessed with ongoing expansion? Expanding by all kinds of illegal means, breaking all kinds of laws and regulations? To the point that the Securities and Exchange Commission is investigating Mosley's entire operation?

My intuition tells me that most likely it is greed.

Among the highest social ranks, extra pressure is on because doing the right thing just doesn't make billions of dollars. The moguls, once famous for their stability and work ethic, are turning into every man for himself, sinking into dog-eat-dog fights.

Greed breeds a "grotesque materialism" which is destroying our morality.

Cheating is now normalized. There is a new national moral standard: 'whatever it takes.' And we have a vast betrayal of the public trust. It is devouring our famous social contract.

Greed is not just a matter of attachment to things; it's attachment to our attachment to things. The need to control others is the obsession that keeps us imprisoned in our greed.

Control of others is the prime trait of an addictive culture. And Mosley is the prime example.

Doing better means earning more money. There can be no doubt that greed and corruption are the cancer of a free society.

There can be no doubt either that powerful and privileged groups profit greatly from maintaining the secret dealings that fill the banks with their loot.

It seems to me that gratitude responds, "Thank you"; Greed demands, "More."

Greed is misery because greed doesn't know the meaning of enough.

And so here we have an incarnation: Mosley is greed. And no one or nothing will get in his way to acquire more and more wealth, power and influence.

How true the axiom that the rich don't get richer and poor poorer, but the rich get richer *because* the poor get poorer

What a horrible existence!

Mosley has all the comforts and luxuries in the world yet no peace of mind, no love, no satisfaction.

Mosley is obsessed by ambition and greed despite what destruction he perpetrates against those who are or are perceived as opponents to his designs and mandates.

I utter a short prayer for him, asking God to show him infinite mercy despite his many sins against the human family and his own family, his daughter.

93

Squeaky is making his report to the Don.

"Dis Charon, he dresses like an old man with a cane. But he goes to the mail box. That's how we know who he is. We are gonna shoot, but he whirls around."

"He got Clop in the heart. Don, he is so fast. He's like a blur."

"On with it, Squeaky," the Don says, obviously annoyed.

"Well, I get a shot off and hit him in the left side. Then he returns fire and gets me in the shoulder as youse can see. My shot trows him off or I'd be dead right now."

"Don, I swear to God in heaven, he rushes out of the Post Office like a scared deer. Outside he puts one right between Josh's eyes. I don't see it, but I seen it after.

"People outside says he runs down the street like a Olympic champion, with a hole in his side!"

"Yur sure you got him in the side?" the Don asks, looking for assurance

"Don, I swear to God in heaven, I got him. I never lie to you. He's wounded."

The Don calls Jigger over. "Jigger, you call every hospital in the city and find out if anybody with a gunshot wound in his left side was dere. Tell dem youse are from the FBI or somethin'.

The Don heaves a deep sigh. "If youse got him, Squeaky, we know he's hurt. At least he won't bother Father Mike any more. But we need to make sure he's not gonna bother anybuddy else.

"How?" Squeaky exclaims.

"I gotta tink on it," the Don says.

99

The presidential campaign is winding down. Three weeks till the election

The hostility between the President and his opponent is as vicious as prehistoric animals in a life and death struggle.

Most of the people aren't even paying attention. The people who are following the campaign are fed up.

There is an actual hatred for the President. He is considered to be a moron, a buffoon, stupid, incompetent.

Ever since the Vice President was assassinated, the Presidency is on a downhill drag like water down a drain.

The President's opponent isn't much better. A blowhard, always mouthing off and saying nothing.

The President seemed to be very comfortable, convinced he would have no trouble defeating his opponent.

There are still rumors that the President himself is behind the assassination of Rick Shayne.

Then ten days before the election, the President does the unbelievable. He signs a wide ranging $555 trillion bill to continue funding the war in Columbia.

It's the camel's straw.

The President is ousted from office in a landside defeat.

The whole matter draws nothing but indifferent yawns. Then it is back to business as usual. No one expected anything from the newly elected President. People would just wait out another four years.

Skip says to me, "How, in this great nation, can't we produce candidates of worth, intelligence and integrity?"

I say back to him, "We won't until we wrest the government out of the stranglehold of the multi nationals like the one headed up by Stanley Mosley. They're the ones who are running the nation."

"I have heard of small groups of billion and trillionaires who decide who will be President.

"They want the weak and the less intelligent for President so they can maneuver and manipulate him or her with the ease of a puppeteer.

"So," Skip says, "these groups would never want someone like Rick Shayne as the President."

"Probably not," I say to him, "but from my sources, I think that integrity and openness and honesty were not Shayne's prominent virtues. He was a behind-the-scenes manipulator. According to these sources, he has been duplicitous, deceitful, and deliberately destructive to the American democracy. A real sneaky type who maneuvered the President like moving a piece on a chess board."

"Remember," I say to Skip, "when Shayne declared himself exempt from a rule that applies to everyone else in the executive branch, instructing the National Archives that the Office of the Vice President is not an 'entity within the executive branch' and therefore is not subject to presidential executive orders."

"It's a screwed up world," Skip sighs and finishes his beer.

חַתַן

I pay my usual monthly visit to Maury Lyons. It should be weekly. I feel guilty. Forever a Catholic!

Maury is blind. He lost his sight when he ran into a burning building to save a child, which he did.

But he can't see anymore as a result.

Maury can still say Mass using Braille. He can still preach. He can still hear confessions.

So the Cardinal allowed him to stay on the job.

The Cardinal didn't have much of a choice since Maury was touted as one of the most valiant heroes in the state, in the country.

His heroic act followed by his blindness made him a prime choice for interviews all over the place.

He played it smooth. Being humbly gracious which only endeared him all the more thousands of people all over the country.

Now that's all gone and he lives in the solitude of darkness. I and a few others are the only ones who stop by to see him.

As they say, Today's headlines are tomorrow's yawn.

He lives as semi retired in St. Pat's downtown. The people love him but they hesitate to show their love as if Maury were some kind of leper.

People are like that with those who have disabilities or deformities. Why I don't know. But that's the way it is.

So much for Christian compassion. The priests of the Archdiocese have all but forgotten Maury since he doesn't get around much.

Maury sits all day and I believe he prays constantly as he whittles pieces of wood into unusually exquisite statuettes. Actually it's not whittling. It's sculpting.

It's really unbelievable when you think he is blind.

On one visit I say to him, "I don't know how you do it," referring to his sculpting.

"Do what?" Maury says smiling gently, indicating that he can't see what he produces.

"Fortunately," he says, "blindness doesn't block creativity. It's just a matter of being flexible and not allowing yourself to be squeezed and squashed into routine and old ways of doing things."

"For instance," he continues, "I can tell what I'm doing by feeling the statuette I'm working on. Then I can picture it in my mind."

"Of course," I say to him, "you were creative before …"

"I lost my sight?" he finishes what I don't want to say.

"We are all creative," Maury says. "It's just that we don't develop our creative powers. For instance," he says, "what you do in solving crimes is a magnificent example of being creative."

"I thank you for that, Maury," I say to him with genuine modesty.

"Any creative person sees the beauty in the ordinary," Maury says. "When you solve a crime, you see the beauty in the result."

"Not always," I say, thinking of Jim, locked up in that mental institution. "Sometimes," I say, "solving a crime can be heartbreaking."

"But isn't heartbreak a form of beauty?" Maury challenges as he always does, leaving me with a puzzle to ponder.

"One of the problems in current preaching," Maury says, more in an academic tone that a judgmental one, is the lack of creativity. They should be using the gospel stories as springboards into creative, imaginative applications to peoples' real stories."

"I fear," I say, "that there isn't the hard work put into preparations for homilies. Too much off the cuff. Not enough thought. And, of course, as far as style, figures of speech and such ... forget it."

"It's a shame," Maury says, "as I said, we all have the ability to be creative, but if we don't use it, we lose it."

It's always refreshing to chat with Maury. I leave him after we bless each other promising to come back oftener. I will.

101

Charon is sitting at table in his run down apartment.

He always takes a room like this. Out of the way. Private. A way of preserving his anonymity.

He has all kinds of medication on the table.

The bullet is too deep for him to dig it out. All he can do is to try to stop the bleeding on the left side of his body.

"Damn," he says to himself, "if I were in France or Belgium, I could go to a hospital," he says to himself.

"Here I am sitting on millions and, if I go to a hospital, they'll contact the police. I can't get a doctor to take this bullet out of me. I don't know any doctor here I can go to."

He winds cloth and tape around his stomach, covering the wound. The blood seems to stop gushing.

He grabs a bottle of bourbon and takes a deep swig.

He never thought he would have been compromised the way the Don had done to him.

Why does the Don want to get me? Who's he working for? He's a known criminal. Why would he want to interfere in my work?

How did that idiot get a shot off? I only wounded him. That never happened before. His shot threw me off balance.

Charon feels the anger rising in him like a geyser. Somehow he's got to find a doctor or nurse to help him.

But he has no idea where to go. In a city the size of Chicago there has to be one doctor who lost his license and for the right amount would take this bullet out of his side.

102

It is early evening and I had just come back from locking up the church.

A lot of pastors lock their doors after the last Mass in the morning. But I like to keep them open so that people can drop in for a visit.

I know I'm taking a risk. But my parish now is in a better neighborhood. Chances are that no one will try to destroy anything.

The doorbell sounds.

I go and look through the peep hole the Cardinal commanded me to have installed.

It's Squeaky.

At first I thought his nickname is due to his shoes, but once I heard him speak, I'm aware of why he's called Squeaky.

I open the door.

"Hello, Squeaky," I say to him, wondering why he would be coming to see me. I'm certain it's not to go to confession.

"Fadder Mike," Squeaky says in his high pitch, "youse gotta come right now. It's the Don.

"The Don?" I say to him.

"I tink he's dying. He asks for youse." Now his voice is trembling. There are tears in his eyes.

I run over to the church and get a host, pick up my oils and come rushing back.

"I got a car waitin,'" Squeaky says.

I get into the car and Squeaky drives like he's in the Indy 500.

"What happened?" I ask Squeaky.

"He was just eatin' and he collapsed on the table. We take him up to his room."

I didn't know the Don lived above the restaurant.

"We call the doctor and he comes and says, 'Heart attack. I warned him about too much pasta.'"

103

I arrive in the Don's bedroom.

"Ah, Father Mike," the Don smiles at me. Thank you for coming. I think this is the end."

"Now, now, Don," I say to him, "you're too mean to die." Thinking of what Scuds said to me about Charon.

The Don gives a short, weak laugh.

"I better get ready to meet the man upstairs," he says, sounding weaker by the moment.

My eyes fill. The Don, for all the cut throat, criminal activities he's been involved in, has always been a gracious and helpful friend.

As he said to me one time, "I like you, Father Mike, you don't judge me."

His last help, trying to get Charon off my trail, is just another sign of the esteem he has always held me in.

"Do you think the man upstairs will understand? That it's just a matter of business?"

How often I hear that! "It's just business." The former prostitutes at Forrow Haven, my departed friend, the magnetic fund raiser, Monsignor Eric Stouffer, killed in my place. The list goes on.

"I'm certain that God in his infinite mercy will understand, Don," I say to him reassuringly.

I believe what I am saying.

I believe that because of the infinite redemptive merits of Jesus, God has already forgiven us every evil we *will* ever do. He does not even wait for us to commit a sin. His forgiveness has already been given to us. With this realization there is no room for fear or despair.

I try to put this thought into words the Don will readily understand. I say to him, "Remember the Prodigal son? His father forgave him before he was even finished with his act of contrition."

The Don sighs. It's relief.

Then the Don gathers what strength he has left and says to me something that is truly profound or I just don't expect to hear from him.

He says, "Here I am, Father Mike, leaving the continuity of life for the inevitability of death. It's the comedy and tragedy of it all.

"Sometimes when we lose ourselves in fear or despair or in barren routine or in fickle hopelessness, we finally find God. And then we share ourselves in soft spoken secrets."

I am astounded. All these years I have known the Don and it's in his last breaths that he reveals his true self to me. That he is a profound thinker -- a theologian!

I usher the men out of the room and hear the Don's confession, anoint him and give him Holy Communion.

"Stay the course, Father Mike," and he closes his eyes to meet 'the man upstairs.'

As I am leaving, Squeaky says to me, "Come back, Fadder Mike, anytime. Youse are always welcome here."

Is Squeaky taking over? With that voice? Squeaky, I assume, is far more treacherous than his voice would indicate.

I doubt that I'll come back. I walk home (my preference), my heart is as heavy as an immovable boulder. My body guards, all four of them, walk with me —close.

I whisper a prayer for my dear friend, the Don, asking God to treat him with good humor.

104

Mosley's trial goes faster than I thought it would.

Mosley has, as is expected, a line up of seven lawyers, all of whom are the cream of the crop. Each of whom have no losses on his resume. Another "Dream Team."

Needless to say, they fight like alley bullies to keep the evidence out. They have citings of other cases galore. Chapter and verse of every conceivable law book.

In the end, the judge makes his decision.

"I find the evidence adduced to be sufficient as a matter of law."

The evidence, every piece of it, is in.

Corruption, theft, kickbacks, bribery as well as for fraud, market manipulation, blackmail, payoffs, insider trading, money laundering. The list is as interminable as a blast off into outer space.

Law and Order who was also in intense attendance leans over to me and says,

"You don't bank billions by playing by the rules."

One piece of evidence I hadn't heard before: bribes to secure contracts with the US government, obtained through the now deceased Vice President, Rick Shayne.

Granted the judge has no patience for the defense attorneys, and they are swimming upstream all the way.

The prosecutors seem almost to be winging it. It is so easy. Evidence after evidence is presented as smoothly as sliding down a snow bank on a toboggan.

I sit there watching and observing.

When it comes to the hiring of an assassin, a multitude of objections are launched, only to be overruled.

The phone tapes are played. There's no doubt about Mosley's plots.

Why would Mosley keep those tapes? Arrogance, sheer, unadulterated arrogance, that and fantasized vanity

He really thinks he's above the law. More powerful than anyone in any kind of power.

Then come the results of the assassin's work. There is a general, loud intake of breath, a loud, spreading gasp of horror, when the part of Mosley's daughter is brought forward.

The judge's face twists into a scowl. He bellows, "Order," and bangs his gavel several times. The defense attorneys look bewildered.

Women in the jury dab their eyes with handkerchiefs. Men stare down at the floor.

Mosley sits straight, his face as immovable as if shaped in plaster of Paris. He looks like he's presiding over a Board meeting where his word will be the final gavel.

As I said, the trial is over almost before it began. A lightning rod of justice.

Several days later: "We find the defendant guilty on all counts," the young woman announces with a bitterness that was like acid on her tongue.

Mosley stands up and is ushered out by the guards. There isn't a sign of anything on his face. His face looks like a smooth stone.

The man is blazingly egocentric; voluptuously calm in an obvious attempt to make his corruption inconspicuous.

One of the prosecutors says to another, "There'll be appeals up the wazoo."

"At least up to the Supreme Count," the other one says.

I overhear this and tend to agree wholeheartedly. Mosley has Senators and Governors in his deep pockets like a kid with a pocket full of marbles.

He's probably already conniving with his lawyers.

Three weeks later the judge sentenced Mosley to life in prison with no possibility of parole.

Unknown to me, somewhere far away, the remaining five members of the group who paid for the Vice President's assassination, look at each other in astonishment. Their leader is headed for prison. What will they do?

Lawrence Oliver Tobin of the Securities and Exchange Commission comes over to me.

"We owe you and your colleague, Mavis Sullivan, big time, Father Mike. Without the evidence you supplied, we would never have nailed this son of … this criminal."

I must admit I do feel a wash of satisfaction. I pray for those whose obsessive ambition causes them to sacrifice so much of what is valuable in themselves and in their lives so that when they fail, there is nothing left inside.

1.75

I'm returning from hospital visitations in the early evening surrounded by my guards. I finally convince them to leave the hospital room when I'm hearing someone's confession.

I tell my guards that it's okay for them to stay outside the rectory.

"Father Skip's inside with his .357 Magnum," I laugh slightly to give the impression that I'm not scared.

My guards aren't happy but they capitulate. They don't want to give me the impression they're suffocating me.

I enter through the back door. Immediately my intuition tells me something's amiss.

I enter the dinning room and switch on the light.

Across the room at the other doorway, Skip is sprawled out with an obvious gun wound in his forehead.

I freeze. I hear heavy breathing. I turn and in the corner is a man slouched down in the opposite corner.

Again my intuition tells me this must be Charon. With a revolver in his hand.

It's been said that when you face death, your whole life streams before you.

That doesn't happen.

There is just a huge knot twisting in my gut like a brutal fist grabbing my stomach.

I try to utter a prayer but to no avail. I think of calling out to my guards, but I'd be dead before they could get in here. Then they would shoot Charon and end his reign of terror.

I was frozen like a giant icicle.

"Father Mike," Charon says in a voice thinner than I would have expected.

I inch a bit closer still anticipating my own murder.

"Father Mike," Charon whines again, "I'm dying."

That's when I saw the wound in his side, oozing blood. "I'll call 911," I say to him.

But he says back to me, "No use, Father Mike, I am dying. It had to happen sooner or later," he tried to laugh, but succeeded only in gasping.

He *is* dying.

He drops his gun to the floor.

I sit down beside him. His blood seeps onto my coat and pants. He's bleeding profusely.

Charon's face is handsomely chiseled. But it was now concrete gray. A full head of black hair. The green pupils of his eyes are fading. I could tell from his outstretched legs that he had to be about six feet three or four inches tall.

"Father Hecken?" I ask pointing over to Skip.

"He came in wielding his magnum. I had to shoot him. Self-defense." Charon's breathing is labored.

"And you got in, how?" I ask, wondering why I'm asking these questions. I don't think I have to establish communication.

"I'm Charon," he smiles with a touch of arrogance like you should ask.

"Out shepherding your flock?" Charon asks with almost a pleasant smile.

"You could say that," I say back to him.

"I know quite a bit about shepherding myself." This time his smile is pleasant.

Suddenly my intuition flashes like that light bulb over a head you see in cartoons.

"You're a pr ..."

1:06

"*Was* a priest," he interrupts.

"How in God's name did you …?

"Become a professional assassin?" he interrupts again, finishing my question.

"It's a long story," he says, "and I don't have much time. I'll give you the edited version, but, Father Mike, I want to make my peace with God before …"

With the latter, he was pleading. First the Don, now Charon. I wonder what other pastors are doing these days.

"It started," Charon says to me, "when I was assigned to an inner city parish.

"The parish environment was an urban jungle. Two major gangs were at constant war with each other, kids getting killed every day. People afraid to leave their homes or come to church. It was unbearable violence.

"So I decide to get involved. I talk to the leaders of each gang. They mock me and show me the door, literally kick me out .

"I thought they'd respect the Roman collar. They don't respect anyone or anything.

"In fact, I am convinced that I became a target, though I couldn't prove it.

"Then one evening I'm taking my little four-year old niece to the ice cream parlor.

"We're walking back to the rectory, eating our ice cream cones, laughing and giggling. Suddenly a car comes zooming by. With my instinct I learned from being in Special Ops. I pulled my niece down to the ground as the bullets flew at us.

"The drive-by kept speeding away. I wasn't hurt, but my niece laid dead in my arms, as cold as the ice cream inert on the pavement.

107

"After my niece's funeral, I went to my attic.

"I took out my Marine M40. My sniper rifle I used when I was in Special Ops.

"I was the best. I have the medals to prove it.

"All I wanted to do was to get revenge. I didn't consider anything else. Not the gospel, not the teachings of the church, not my conscience.

"I went out that night into the streets. I shot and killed the leaders of both gangs. It was in all the papers and on the TV news programs.

"They were comparing me to Charles Bronson, you know, in those movies. Some were calling me a vigilante, others a serial killer.

"The whole place was in an uproar. It was tumultuous. I sat in front of my TV watching all day. I felt in control, satisfied, good.

"The next night I went out again. This time I killed five from one gang and seven from the other.

"The police were screaming that they would get me and soon.

"At last I killed off all the members of both gangs. People came out of their houses and danced in the streets. They booed the police when they showed up. Peace was restored. Peace through violence, but peace.

"My anonymity had been preserved. I packed up and left my parish. I thought I'd look for another urban hell hole and clean it up.

"Then it dawned on me. I have a marketable skill. I could sell my services. And so I did. I took the name Charon and, as they say, the rest is history."

I sit listening intently, mesmerized by Charon's brief tale. There must be much more to his story, but, as Charon said, his time is running out.

"What about the innocent people you took out?" I asked.

"Somebody thinks they weren't innocent."

"You mean like the Vice President?" I ask gingerly.

"For all your sleuthing, you missed one glaring fact: the Vice President was the scum of the earth.

"A five million dollar job, that one," he sort of scowled. "My clients composed a long list of reasons why the Vice President should not be allowed to run for President."

I couldn't figure if he was experiencing distaste for "the job" or regret that he would never be able to spend the money.

I would have loved to pursue "the job" but time is running out.

But I do ask, "What about Joey?"

"It had to be. My anonymity had to be preserved at all costs. I'm not a homosexual. It just happened. I fell in love with him and he with me. Believe me, sending Joey to his grave is the most heartbreaking thing I've ever done. I still weep over it. You see, I still have a conscience."

"But," I insist, "why were you coming after me. You killed Joey."

"Maybe to make an example of you. You know, don't try to mess with Charon.

259

At this point now, I realize it was a silly vendetta. A waste ..."

His voice is fading in and out. He doesn't have much time left. The great terrorist Charon will soon be no more.

108

"One more thing, Father Mike ..."

"Yes," I say with no little trepidation. I still don't know if he still intends to carry out his threat on me. You can never tell.

"In my wallet, in the secret compartment, is the name of my Swiss bank and my bank number. The same for my Caribbean bank. There are millions. I want you to take it and use it for charity. It might buy me some time out of Purgatory."

"I'd rather not," I say.

"You'd deny a dying man his final wish?"

I don't answer.

"My confession?" Charon asks as if he's worried that I might deny that final wish too.

After he confesses, I give him absolution.

"I'm so sorry," he whispers. So sor ..."

He closes his eyes. Charon's vendetta dies with him.

I call in my guards. They're a mess, trying to figure out what happened in my dinning room. They check me because of the blood they see on my coat and pants. They are satisfied that I'm okay.

They call the Coroner to come for the bodies.

I call the Cardinal to tell him about Skip. I get his voice mail. I tell him Skip's dead and I'll explain everything to him tomorrow.

The guards have no idea that the man lying dead in the corner of the room is Charon. I don't tell them. Why? I'm not sure.

109

I go upstairs to change and shower off the blood. For some reason I feel heavy-hearted.

I'm certainly suffering loss over Skip's death. He is – was—such a good friend. Such a support. And now …

I don't know if I'm saddened because of the devastation Charon caused under the rubric of restoring justice and peace.

Or if I'm distressed because Charon is – was – a priest. One of us. One who stood at the altar and changed bread and wine into the Body and Blood of Jesus Christ. One who sat in a confessional and forgave sins.

Then he elects to choose a life of murdering for money. Millions he said.

I sit down, light my pipe and pour myself a stiff one. I still feel myself trembling.

"Peace through violence," I ponder Charon's words.

How often throughout history has that been used to excuse the violence unleashed on human beings?

I didn't even get his real name. Father who?

Is there peace through violence? That's the part of Charon's story I wanted to ask about: did the environment at his urban parish remain peaceful? Or did other gangs take over after he left?

I have never believed in any kind of violence. I admit I take some pride in following or trying to follow the non violent Christ.

I have always believed that we have to be very careful not to blame violence entirely on outside diabolical forces. You know, "the devil made me do it." If we do this, we will shift the blame for violence away from ourselves. The reality is that we all have the capacity to be violent.

Power corrupts and the corruption is violence. The ruthless disregard for others is violence. Even if that power is of parents over children, teachers over students, churchmen over congregations.

Insensitivity is also a viable form of violence.

There may be more violence in manipulation than in physical abuse.

The violence of the psychopath is obvious; it's the violence of the so-called normal person that is far more dangerous.

מוב

I remember seeing a movie on television a few years ago entitled "Jacobo Timerman: Prisoner Without a Name." The movie traced what happened to a fearless Argentine newspaper publisher, Jacobo Timerman, when he took extraordinary risks to speak out against a totalitarian military regime.

It was a horror story of false accusations, imprisonment without trial, torture without remorse and finally the arbitrary cancellation of his citizenship and deportation from his homeland.

It was a movie about violence. Not only the physical torment which we ordinarily associate with the term, violence, but a violence that dug down deep into the human spirit and tore to shreds any hope for reform.

Then there was the prophet, Archbishop Romero who spoke for the God not of the powerful and the wealthy. Nor was his the domesticated God of the middle class. He spoke for the God of the poor, the downtrodden, the marginalized, the enslaved.

This made him a dangerous opponent of those who held the poor in bondage.

He spoke out against not only the greed of individuals but the greed of sinful social structures which so often create consumer societies run wild. As Pope Paul challenged, "In a consumer society we must decide if we are spending or squandering."

"At the base of all violence," Archbishop Romero said, "is social injustice, accurately called 'structural violence' which is our greatest social evil today."

Romero also said, "As Christians we must condemn this structure of sin in which we live, this corruption, this disorder of selfishness and social injustice."

His was a dangerous voice and, like the Hebrew prophets before him, his voice was ruthlessly silenced by the guardians of "structural violence."

But a martyr's blood leaves an indelible stain on the cover-up for injustice.

I still cannot understand why Romero hasn't been formally canonized. The powers of the Vatican say they're trying to decide if the Archbishop was killed for the faith or because of political reasons.

Talk about splitting hairs. Those Vatican careerists really need to get a life or at least a priestly life.

What about the first martyrs in the church? Weren't their deaths a mix of faith and politics? For example, Nero's persecution.

111

With all due respect for Archbishop Romero, his countercultural stance was against the violence of those who impoverish the peasants and keep them prisoners of poverty.

And even though Charon is – was – a violent assassin, there are other forms of violence.

I find that in the spiritual life perfectionism is a form of violence. Well meaning people who allow themselves to be controlled by the scrupulous observance of letter of the law. That's violence they visit on themselves.

On the other hand, the despotic controlling others is a form of violence.

But we seldom think of these as violence and that's what makes perfectionism and control so insidious.

Someone said that the drug of choice for adults and teens today is violence.

It would seem that people in our modern, sophisticated society are addicted to one form of violence or another.

As soon as the word, violence, is mentioned, we usually think of war, oppression, torture, muggings, murder, abused children, battered wives.

But just as there is white collar crime, so there is the whited sepulcher of violence. Violence made to look tolerable by whitewashing it with the claim that it is merely a venial sin or for the less religious, a matter of National Security, that catch-all that is used to excuse the most gruesome acts of violence under the saluted flag.

The obvious acts of physical violence often blind us to the violence disguised as acceptable social behavior.

But not all violence is physical.

Isn't there the violence of losing one's temper and lobbing verbal bombs at another person, blasting him or her into the pit of worthlessness?

Aren't rash judgments, false accusations, self-righteous condemnations, back-stabbing defamation of another's character, the silent treatment, slandering another's reputation, so-called harmless gossip all acts of violence?

Aren't taking advantage of another, crushing someone to get ahead, disregard for the dignity of students, family members, neighbors, fellow parishioners, flagrant abuse of authority, arrogant indifference toward legitimate authority acts of violence?

Isn't deliberate refusal to work on and enhance our own self-esteem, self-worth, self-acceptance violence?

Isn't destruction of land or the careless pollution that pockmarks the very earth that sustains our existence violence?

The problem is that these acts occur with such regularity and are done by so many that they are never thought of as being violent. That is, unless we are on the receiving end.

No, there can never be peace through violence.

112

I shake myself out of my reverie.

It's time to call Detective Alison Masconi. We need to talk about Charon. Talk is all we can do, now that he's dead.

Alison comes over the next morning.

"Hi, Detective," I say to her.

"I really think it's time to call me Alison," she says with a pretty, almost flirtatious, smile.

Or was I just imagining a flirtation. God help me and bless celibacy. For a split second I wonder what it would be like to be married to Alison. I immediately put the thought out of mind. God bless celibacy.

"Let me run something past you," I say to her.

She immediately drops what I consider her coquetry and gives me her total attention.

"I'm thinking or more it's my intuition that we should keep Charon's death quiet at least for the present."

Alison's eyes flash open. "Why?" she exclaims.

"I don't know. I just have this gut feeling that for some elements, if they think Charon is still around, it may be a restraint. You know, Charon as a threat."

"With due respect," Alison says, "that just doesn't make sense."

"Can you trust me on this?" I ask her.

"It's a big leap for me," she retorts.

"Of course, I'll have to tell the Cardinal. But he'll keep it as confessional.

"What if he orders you to reveal that Charon is dead?" she persists.

"He won't," I say with the self assurance of a soothsayer. "The Cardinal puts all his trust in my judgment."

"Must be very tidy to have that kind of security," she says almost with envy in her voice. Envy because she doesn't have that same kind of security.

"I know this from past experiences," I say to her.

"I still don't know why you don't want to let it be known that Charon is dead and gone."

"Like I said, I'm not quite sure either. I just have this, well, for want of a better word, this itch that keeps calling my attention back to not revealing."

"If I don't tell my bosses, I could get into a lot of trouble," she's not going to let it go.

"Actually, I don't think I told you directly that Charon is dead. I just said maybe we should keep his death quiet."

"You priests, you're worse than lawyers when it comes to twisting words to fit your plots.

"Okay, I'll keep it quiet, but you had better decide to make it public soon."

We stand and embrace. She smells so good, so inviting. Her hug is a clinging to.

Am I just imagining all this? I don't know.

God bless celibacy.

113

I have no doubt that Cheron was sincerely sorry.

But then again, he might have been a sociopath.

If so, how responsible was he?

This is a problem I am wrestling with for years.

I have even done some study on the matter. My priest brothers think I'm a geek, I know. But I just have this insatiable curiosity.

I even have notes in my computer. So I turn to it now.

Sociopathy is a mental disease. The essential feature is a pervasive disregard or, even the violation of, the rights of others. Considered essential features of this disorder are compulsiveness and manipulation. There is no regret of conscience.

Just from that brief entry, it seems that to diagnose someone as a sociopath is complex.

Something I'm not equipped to unravel.

But, as you may have guessed, what is of interest to me is the matter of responsibility and accountability for a person's actions.

If an individual is a sociopath, then he or she is suffering from a mental disease, a psychological disorder.

And if he or she is sick, how responsible is he or she for his or her actions?

What is really the Gordian knot is just how much responsibility there is?

Certainly, according to his own words, Charon made a deliberate choice to take up his sniper rifle to kill those gang mobsters.

Certainly, he made a conscious choice to sell his "skill" and become a professional assassin. But was there a moment when he no longer was making responsible choices? When he ceased being rational? When his compulsiveness took over and his conscience was no more in charge of his decisions and actions than his breathing?

Obviously, Charon had invested all his existential capital in a permanent, endless stream of an unmanageable cause.

His brutal battle had been with the inadequacies of the cumbersome bureaucracy of the Establishment.

He had undoubtedly been caught between his twisted convictions and failed grace.

Anyway he had enough rage to drown all of us in a sea of blood.

The fact that Charon wanted to make his peace with God through confession tells me that he wasn't a sociopath. He had a conscience. A sociopath has no idea what a conscience is. Has no sense whatsoever of right and wrong.

I don't know why I keep gnawing on this problem like a hungry dog. It brings back horrible memories of Jim.

Jim's is a easy call. Charon's much more complicated.

But under the law a person is fully responsible for his or her actions. And after all the philosophical meanderings, the law is what stands as firmly as if in concrete.

I should just let God judge. Who can fathom the human mind? Not to mention the human psyche or the moral responsibility of an individual?

I'll just keep Charon in my prayers as I do Jim who murdered all those prostitutes. The thought of Jesus being condemned comes to mind. In the midst of the religious leaders' howls of damnation, Jesus smiled salvation.

It's like when I preach. I have to admit I don't know what everyone seated in front of me is going through. A married couple on the verge of divorce, trying to keep up appearances; parents of a son or daughter who has given up on faith and living wantonly; a child who is sick with an undiagnosed disease.

But what I do believe is that these people need a closer intimacy with God who inspires them to reach out to others with concern and love. So that's how I preach.

And so I must conclude that Charon's was a clumsy salvation.

114

Just when things are settled, I get a phone call.

It's Mavis. And she sounds hysterical.

"Mavis! What is it?" I yell through the phone.

"Oh, Father Mike!" Mavis cries. "Oh, Father Mike!"

"Mavis, please calm down and tell me ..."

"A man with a gun came into Farrow Haven ..." she pauses to catch her breath.

"A man with a gun?" I ask.

Mavis seems a bit more in control now.

"He just opened fire ... three of the girls are dead, including young Maisie. Oh, Father Mike, it was horrible."

"And you, Mavis? Are you okay?" I ask, my anxiety rising like blood rushing to my head. In fact, I do feel dizzy. Almost afraid to hear Mavis' answer.

"He got me in the left arm. I'm calling from the hospital. St. Luke's."

"Mavis, stay there. I'll be there in a few minutes and take you home."

Home? What a strange word for Forrow Haven. It's not really Mavis' home. She has her own apartment, but she's subletting it.

And now, her "home" has been invaded by another assassin.

This assassin doesn't have Charon's skills. Charon would have taken Mavis out and not shot anyone else.

There's no doubt in my mind that Mavis is the target. Mosley found out or knows she's the one responsible for the evidence against him, the evidence who put him in prison for life with no possibility for parole.

There's no doubt that Mosley's behind this. He's vindictiveness incarnate.

What now?

When Mosley finds out that Mavis is still alive, he'll hire another hit man. He still has enough wealth to wield his power and influence.

As soon as I bring Mavis back to Forrow Haven, I must contact Detective ... Alison.

I'll take a chance and drop by her office.

115

"But, Father Mike, you have no proof," Alison exclaims, sounding as if she were a teacher scolding a student who should know better.

I stand in her office wishing I had called her on the phone.

"Who else would want to kill Mavis?" I retort with some petulance.

"Father Mike, Mavis was only wounded. It could have been a pimp, furious at one of his girls who deserted him."

I couldn't deny that Alison has a point. Maybe I do jump to my conclusion too fast. Maybe I want it to be Mosley. Still there is my intuition ...

Yet, if it is a pimp and "one of his girls," why did he kill two others? Especially little Maisie?

So I pursue the same argument with Alison that I had with myself earlier.

"Suppose Mosley is behind this. When he finds out that Mavis wasn't eliminated, won't he hire another hit man to take her out?

"Must Mavis live the rest of her life looking over her shoulder? Living in fear each and every day?

"I am responsible. I'm the one who persuaded her to go to Mosley's office and get all that evidence. And she got far more evidence than I couldn't even think of.

"So I feel obliged to do something to protect her. And I'm going on my intuition that Mosley's behind these murders."

"You're stubborn as a mule," Alison smiles in that coquettish way. There it goes again. That feeling I haven't had in years. That feeling I thought I had under total control.

But right now, I feel the excitement of a teenager getting a date with the most popular girl in the class.

For an instant, my memory goes back to the girl in eighth grade. Call it puppy love if you will. But, as far as I'm concerned, I was in love. And I think she had serious feelings for me.

We never did anything bad. We kissed several times but, as they say, it was like kissing my sister.

Then I went off to the seminary and she moved – far away. And that was that.

Now here I am with the same unruly feelings toward Alison.

I'm reading into this far too much. Alison would be horrified if I ever expressed what I am feeling.

She might even call me a dirty old man. After all, there has to be thirty years between us.

Oh well, back to the business at hand.

"Alison, you're the detective. Following my intuition, what can we do?"

"We could go to the District Attorney and tell him about your hunch. If he doesn't laugh us out of his office, he may approach a judge."

"Or," I say, sounding quite the sage, "we could go to Law and Order Tobin. After all, he owes us. He said so."

"Leave it to you, Mike. You always have an angle." Again that smile. *And* for the second time she called me Mike, not Father Mike.

This time I fell myself reacting with an almost boyish thrill like a Freshman in high school.

116

Lawrence Oliver Tobin is most gracious.

He hasn't heard of the massacre at Forrow Haven.

He's shocked, to say the least.

"My God!" he exclaims, who, what …?"

I never saw Law and Order so discombobulated.

Alison speaks up.

"I think it could have been an angry pimp. Father Mike here thinks it's Mosley reaching out through prison bars and putting a contract out on Mavis Sullivan.

"I think my take is more practical, but then Father Mike's version makes sense too. And if it is Mosley, he'll sure enough put out another contract. There can be no doubt that Mosley's vindictiveness is insatiable."

Law and Order sits there, obviously impressed with Alison's brief but comprehensive summary of the views on the tragedy.

I must admit that I too am moved with admiration. Alison's one of a kind. Pretty, bright, in control, incisive, upbeat. She's someone any man would be a hundredfold blessed to have and to hold till death etc.

"So why come to me?" Law and Order asks, sounding a bit defensive as if he knew what we are going to ask of him and not wanting to hear it.

"Assuming that Father Mike's version is closer to the truth," Alison said, "what we need is clout."

"Clout?" Law and Order sounded skittish.

117

"I'm thinking," I say slowly, deliberately so as not to scare Law and Order off, "that if Mosley has outside contacts, he's able to hire a hit man."

"Charon?" Law and Order asks.

"No," I say, "Charon would have taken Mavis out without killing the others. This guy is an amateur. But just as lethal."

I don't tell him Charon's dead. What's the matter with me?

"So," Law and Order says hesitantly as if he's afraid of what he is going to say, "you want me to plug his channels of contact."

"Yes," Alison exclaims with that enthusiasm that is recently her hallmark.

"We are thinking," I say, "of solitary confinement."

"Lord," Law and Order says as deliberately as I am speaking, "I don't know if we can pull this off. Where's the basis besides your hunch or intuition, Father Mike?"

"If Mosley can make contact outside the prison, there is a good chance that Mavis could be murdered," I say to him as persuasively as trying to get a child to take a bath.

Law and Order picks up the phone and calls Special FBI Agent Sylvester Kerns.

He explains the whole matter beginning with the killings at Forrow Haven to our suggestion of solitary confinement.

Then Law and Order listens for what seems like an interminable length of time. Finally he hangs up and turns to us.

"Syl says it's worth a visit to the Warden's office. I'll call you later and let you know how it turns out.

With that he leaves us looking at each other as if we had just been visited by Santa Claus.

118

Later that day Law and Order calls us and invites us over to his office.

I suggest we meet at the Indian Garden restaurant.

He agrees.

"Well?" Alison asks as we're seated.

"Well," Law and Order has a quirky smile on his face, "we did it."

Alison actually applauds and I reach over and shake his hand.

"Details, details," Alison urges with that enthusiasm that is her recent hallmark.

"Well at first," Law and Order seems to be dragging it out, teasing, "the Warden is reluctant. He says, 'On what basis? His lawyers will bombard me. They'll sue everybody including the President.'"

"Then Syl says, 'If he's in solitaire, he won't be able to contact his lawyers.'

"But," the Warden says, 'his lawyers can demand to see Mosley. I can't refuse them.'"

"But," I say to the Warden, 'you can keep it to just one lawyer. Then we can bird dog him – or her – in case Mosley is contacting an assassin through that lawyer.'"

"The Warden says, 'We'll, no, make that, *I'll* be breaking all kinds of laws.'"

"Syl says, 'I'll cover that. The FBI has ways.'"

"I still don't have grounds to toss him into solitaire," the Warden whines.

"Then Syl says, 'I'll tell you what, Warden, have one of your guards get into a confrontation with Mosley. Then swoop in, blame Mosley and throw him into the pit.'"

"Then the Warden asks, 'How long do I keep him there.'"

"I say, 'Out of sight, out of mind. If Mosley does engineer the murder of Mavis Sullivan, you don't want her death traced back to you who was warned ahead of time.'"

"The Warden says, 'Mosley's lawyers are bound to approach a judge to get him out of confinement.'"

"So," I say to the Warden, 'Let him out, arrange another confrontation and throw him back in. Over and over, if necessary.'"

"The man in the iron mask," the Warden says.

"Syl says, 'If needs be. This man is just too treacherous, too vicious to be allowed any kind of freedom to exert his vindictiveness on his enemies. And Mavis Sullivan and probably Father Mike are now his prime enemies.'"

"Finally, the Warden agrees. He says, 'Mosley's powerful but in here I'm *the* power.'"

"Extremely well done," I say to him.

Alison is staring at Law and Order with no less than adoration.

Is this jealousy I'm feeling? God, what's happening to me? I've got to get a hold of myself. For God's sake, I'm a *priest*! God bless celibacy.

119

Mavis is now in charge of Farrow Haven.

She doesn't have to fear Mosley.

One day when Mosley got out of solitaire for a few hours, he actually picks a fight with another lifer. The lifer breaks Mosley's neck.

The only conclusion I can make is that Mosley preferred to die rather than spend more time in confinement.

My conclusion is reinforced by Law and Order and Alison.

It is a tragic end of a tragic life. I really mean this.

I feel somewhat responsible. Not that it's my idea to have Mosley put into solitary confinement and kept there.

Still I certainly supported the plan.

I just couldn't believe that a man as miserly, self-aggrandizing, powerful would ever want to end his life.

No doubt being confined as he was took its toll.

I guess you can never tell.

John of the Cross was confined in a solitary cell for a lengthy time and became a saint.

Anyway Mavis is breathing much more evenly now. The ladies have settled down after that massacre. Of course, they're still grieving especially for young Maisie who had become a kind of pet.

The ladies were using their newly acquired skills to teach Maisie and, as they all agreed, she was a very alert student, learning quickly.

The ladies were so thrilled that they would be able to steer Maisie in the right path of virtue instead of the life they had left behind (I hope).

Mavis is especially grieving for Maisie and the other two women who were so wantonly killed.

She blames herself since she is convinced that the hit man was sent to kill her.

I'm trying to soothe her scruples. I don't know how much success I'm having but I'm hanging in there.

I myself am grieving for Maisie. She was such a heroic little girl. And I was so happy that she took to Forrow Haven so well and was progressing as rapidly as she was.

Haven't heard from Alison lately. She's probably off on another case. One I'm not involved in. Thank God. Have much work to do here in my parish.

God bless celibacy.

My new Parochial Vicar, Jim, is a nice young man. Filled with zeal. Eager to work hard. He sort of reminds me of the Energizer Bunny,

Pleasant to be around. Clever sense of humor.

Thank God for all his blessings to me and through me to others.

120

I have my visit with the Cardinal.

I tell him Charon is dead

He tells me to notify the authorities at once.

Won't Alison be happy to hear how much the Cardinal backs me up!

I don't go into why I was keeping it a secret. Mainly because I just don't know.

The Cardinal is drop-jaw stunned when I tell him Charon was a priest.

"Good Lord!" he exclaimed.

Then he sits back, knowing that I know the story and will be telling him the story.

Which of course I do.

"My God!" he exclaims. "Did you give him absolution?"

"Yes I did," I say to him.

The Cardinal is quiet for what seems a hour; it is only a few minutes.

"That part," he says, "you don't tell the authorities or anyone else. As far as you are concerned, it's confessional."

"With all my high level contacts," the Cardinal heaved his usual sigh, "I think we'll never find out who he was. Maybe that's for the best."

"What evil there is in this world," the Cardinal is truly moved. "There is nothing so vile as the self righteousness of the pious and self-sufficiently orthodox. There is nothing so violent as the people who perpetrate violence with a clear conscience."

"I know," I sigh. "I've seen dead or mangled bodies of those who have been murdered or tortured until they are intermittent nightmares."

"I'm sure you have," he says without judgment.

"But, Cardinal," I say, "I've also seen or witnessed so much good. This is what keeps me going."

"I'm sure that's true," a slight smile which I take as affirmation.

"Just the other day," I say, "I read that in the work of Habitat for Humanity, there were 600,000 volunteer hours and $200 million in charitable grants.

"Yes, yes, I read that too."

"Then," I say, "there are the thousands – millions – who get no headlines for raising their children with gospel values or slave as do one parent families to support their children or those who devote their time to caring for those who are in need, not necessarily financially but in need of support and affirmation when they're down and out."

"You've got me there, Mike," the Cardinal says. "Living here in the stratosphere of the episcopy doesn't allow for much contact with the ordinary members of my flock. That's why when the occasions arise, I try to give my full attention to each one who approaches me."

"And they appreciate it, I can assure you of that," I affirm.

"Cardinal," I say to him with the sincerity of the debtor who owed five hundred silver pieces, "I want to thank you for the guards you supplied."

'You're my priest, Mike," he says. "And you are one of my most treasured."

Well, talk about affirmation! Most treasured! I'm floating.

We bless each other and he says to me, "Thank you, Mike, for all the good you are doing in the vineyard."

121

Sometimes in the evening when I turn off the news on my TV and sit in the shade of eventide my thoughts wander back to the problem of evil.

This evening my thoughts are probably stimulated by my conversation with the Cardinal.

I don't know why I bother with this problem.

It's more than a problem. It's a mystery.

Still my intuitive powers seem to want to grind away like a dog with a bone.

And yet evil is not a mystery when it comes to a man like Mosley.

He chose his path through life as did Charon.

Both paths were evil. Yet in each case, the "chooser" was convinced or had convinced himself that somehow his path was one of righteousness.

Mosley was just making a living. Charon was just fighting evil. That one's sheer irony.

At least that's probably how they rationalized it.

Like Hitler and Stalin. How they had to rationalize!

Like our own government. Who can plumb the depths of our elected leaders' rationalizations? There are times when it seems the government, the nation, is run on the principle, if it could be called that, What they don't know, won't hurt them.

Speaking of which, I called Law and Order and told him Charon is dead. I know he will be thrilled to break the news.

I don't give him many details so that he can feel free to keep me out of it.

He is thrilled. He deserves it.

Getting back to the problem of evil, it's possible that the rationalizations are themselves the real evil.

People with a false consciousness think they're doing the right thing when it is in fact objectively evil.

If nothing else, evil people hate the light because it reveals themselves to themselves; they hate goodness because it reveals their badness; they hate love because it reveals their indifference.

I know from my own experience in dealing with evil that truly evil people actively avoid extending themselves; rather they exert all their efforts to preserve the integrity of their sick selves.

There really are people who respond with hatred in the presence of goodness and would destroy the good insofar as it is in their power to do so.

I guess, after all, evil isn't that much of a mystery.

Perhaps the mystery is why evil exists in the first place.

I guess the question really is: why does God permit evil?

And that question is tied into the gift of our freedom.

God doesn't permit evil. God gives us freedom to choose good or evil and will not interfere with our choices.

That's how much God, the Creator, respects the freedom he has given us.

Oh well, another day.

122

Christine Joyce's wedding is something out of a fashion magazine.

She has fourteen bridesmaids.

All women from Forrow Haven. Mavis Sullivan is her matron of honor.

What a wonderful tribute to the work of that refuge.

McClan Dorrister, the orthopedic surgeon, Christine's fiancé, seems quite satisfied with Christine's arrangement.

He has fourteen doctors lined up and his brother as best man.

My homily ran a bit long:

The pastor was asked to come and talk to the fifth grade about marriage.

The kindly pastor began with a question. "Boys and girls, can any of you tell me what Jesus had to say about marriage?"

There was an awkward silence, the children pretending to think when all they were doing was trying to escape being called on.

Then Johnny came alive like a Roadrunner cartoon. His hand shot up almost piercing the ceiling. He bounced in his seat as if he were on a hot griddle. Breathlessly he called out, "Father, Father!"

"Yes, Johnny," the pastor smiled benignly. "What did Jesus say about marriage?"

"Jesus said, 'Father, forgive them, for they know not what they do.'"

I am certain that today Christine and McClan know exactly what they are doing today.

And in the name of everyone here, I thank them for asking us to participate in the public proclamation of their love sealed with the Sacrament of Matrimony.

In our gospel story, Jesus pronounces no miraculous words over the jugs of water. The water, in a poet's words, simply blushed in the presence of divine power. No words to his mother about what he is going to do either.

But we can imagine a smile as glorious as the sun lighting up Mary's face, even though, as Simeon had predicted, a sword of sorrow pierces her heart as she realizes that Jesus' hour had come.

Then in the seclusion of the off stage scenario, Jesus' voice breaks the silence like a drum roll, Take this and let the head waiter taste it.

The symbol in our gospel story is that the natural was raised to the supernatural level. Water into wine symbolizes how the natural love between you, Christine and McClan can be transformed into divine love.

St. John in his first letter says, God is love. Since God is love, the bond of love between you, Christine and McClan, _is_ God. This is a profound revelation worthy of your lifelong contemplation.

Your love for each other is not just a magnetic emotional pull or a breathless infatuation. Your love for each other is God.

Christine and McClan, it is your challenge to change the water of a humdrum relationship into the wine of a rich, deep, refreshing love.

You can break through the humdrum by open, honest communication, and, surprisingly, even heated disagreements can be the source of a warm, healing bond.

Anyone who is involved in love knows that it's so easy to say, I love you. But loving is hard work.

For example, there are the struggles to overcome barriers of personality differences. There are the bridges to be built over the pitfalls of criticisms. There are the tunnels that have to be burrowed through mountains of each other's personal preferences and pursuits. There is the effort to open the heavy doors that are closed on self-revelatory communication.

The wonderful, truly marvelous aspect of this gospel story is that it's not just an event that happened in Jesus' lifetime but that here and now Jesus, through this sacrament, is continually giving you his power to change the water of taking each other for granted or even indifference into the wine of being passionately involved and selflessly concerned for each other in friendly and supportive mutual love.

Our prayer for you today, Christine and McClan is that Jesus who is Love itself will help you each day to change the water of the usual into the wine of the spectacular.

123

The reception is held in the Dartmouth Country Club, the most exclusive club in all of Chicago.

McClan has his contacts and memberships.

Christine will have no problem adapting to his lifestyle.

She was well on her way to becoming a millionaire when she left everything to take over Forrow Haven.

I just can't say enough about her. Her willingness to give herself to others in big and small ways.

A prayer life that has to be mystical.

Her generosity with her time; her self-sacrificial interpersonal relationships.

In my humble estimation she is the stuff saints are made of.

I remember reading an insight from Archbishop Fulton Sheen.

He said, "As only a wise person can impart wisdom so only a saintly person can communicate sanctity."

And, to my way of thinking anyway, Christine communicates if not sanctity, certainly holiness of life.

She doesn't wear her holiness on her sleeve. It's just her quiet, unobtrusive way of caring for those in need, especially the women of Forrow Haven.

The fact that she included all of them in her wedding entourage proves my point.

I know she will be keeping an eye on Forrow Haven, helping Mavis without trying to still be in charge.

In the final analysis, it's not ecstasies or levitations or miracle working that are the hallmark of saints.

It's dedication to duty always leaving an opening for doing more.

It's refraining from judging, not to mention, condemning others, but accepting people for who they are and where they are and who they can become.

It's kneeling and washing the feet of those you are leading, while laying down your life for those you are serving.

And Christine is the one person who fits all these categories like a hand in a glove.

I offer a prayer of thanks for all the good people I've been blessed to know and to experience.

124

I was happy to see that Alison is also a participant in the wedding celebration.

She finally makes her way over to me.

"Hello, Mike," she says in that dreamy, languorous way of hers.

"Hello, Alison," I say back to her, trying to make sure I'm not showing any discomfiture.

"A beautiful wedding," she says.

"Yes, it was," I say.

"Your sermon or homily was stupendous. A lot to think about. A wonderful take on the Wedding Feast of Cana."

"You are certainly a man with God in his mouth," she smiles as her cheeks turned ruddy.

"May I have a copy?" She is very sincere.

"Thank you. I always appreciate any affirmation that comes my way. And you most certainly will have a copy. Not too many ask for that," I say with sincere modesty.

"Mike," Alison says, lowering her voice almost to the point of being conspiratorial, "I have some news for you."

"Oh," I say. "And what would that be?" I smile probably because she's suddenly so serious.

"Law and Order Tobin has offered me a position at the Securities and Exchange Commission and I've decided to take it. It's such a tremendous opportunity. A real promotion."

"That's wonderful," I say to her, while feeling more than a prickling pain in my gut.

"That's something I'll bet you weren't banking on," I say, hoping I'm not giving away my true feeling.

"No way," she exclaims with almost the impetuous glee of a gymnast. "Law and Order -- I guess I'll have to stop calling him that – told me he likes the way I handle myself, my ability to get to the core of a problem and articulate it."

"I asked him," she still sounded breathless, 'What about solutions?' "He laughed and said, 'If we can set up the problem, the solution is sure to follow.'"

I don't say that I'm not so sure about Law and Order's logic, but I don't want to rain on Alison's parade.

"I'm sure he's right," I finally say to her.

"You know I'll have to move to D.C."

"I figured that," I say.

"Look, Mike, we'll still stay in contact? We'll still be close friends? Chicago and Washington are just a couple of puddle jumps from each other."

"Of course," I say reassuringly.

I must admit that I'm flattered that Alison wants to stay in touch. Maybe she does have some feelings for me. Maybe it wasn't just my imagination.

Then again, it's déjà vu all over again.

My eighth grade sweetheart said something along those same lines before she moved away. "We'll always be in contact," she said.

And I haven't heard from her in a zillion years!

God bless celibacy.

About the

Author

Father T. Ronald Haney is a retired priest from the Roman Catholic diocese in Harrisburg, PA.

He has been a Principal of a high school, a pastor and the Executive Editor for 30 years of *The Catholic Witness*, the diocesan newspaper.

He is a published essayist, poet and novelist. Besides his novels, he has published books on the spiritual life: *God Within You, One Minute Meditations, The Jesus Story, The Stations of Cross, Prayers for Priests.*

He lives in St. Theresa parish, New Cumberland, PA. He can be contacted at: <u>frhaney@hbgdiocese.org</u>

Printed in the United States
205681BV00001B/85-105/P